"Good God,"

"No!" June said urgently. "No, that's not what I meant. Listen to me, Alex." She broke free of his grasp and raised her hands to his cheeks, forcing him to meet her eyes. "It's not your fault. The person to blame is the one who killed Iain. But you have to see...you have to realize...it could have been you. And the note...maybe it was supposed to be you."

Her brilliant blue gaze held fire and courage and something else he was afraid to define. He wrapped his arms around her and held on, drawing strength from her warmth, her slender softness. That he might have unwittingly been the means of Iain's death shook him to his core. Years of friendship and respect, blasted away by a bullet. He wasn't sure he could bear the guilt.

"Come to me." He murmured in her ear. "Come to me tonight." His mouth seared a hot, moist path along her jawline. He needed her, but he realized with wonder it wasn't simply sexual. It was also the desire for comfort and companionship, a sharing of sorrow.

The uneasiness icing his veins was consumed in the flame of passion. Unable to deny himself another taste of her, his lips met hers fiercely, grinding against her teeth until her mouth opened and their tongues twisted together, twirling, teasing. He crushed her against his body, hands sliding from buttocks to shoulders, melding her to fit him. "I need you, June." Desperation filled him, undeniable and indefensible. "It's your call. Your decision. But I want you so bad. I..." he faded to a stop, pressed his mouth to hers once more. "Come to me."

Her breath trembled out. He held her so close he could see his reflection in her eyes. She nodded. "Tonight."

Lori –

Mountain Fire

by

Brenda Margriet

Happy Reading
to my best-est sister!

Brenda Margriet

This is a work of fiction. Names, characters, places, and incidents are either the product of the author's imagination or are used fictitiously, and any resemblance to actual persons living or dead, business establishments, events, or locales, is entirely coincidental.

Mountain Fire

Contact Information: info@thewildrosepress.com

Cover Art by *Tamra Westbury*

The Wild Rose Press, Inc.
PO Box 708
Adams Basin, NY 14410-0708
Visit us at www.thewildrosepress.com

Publishing History
First Crimson Rose Edition, 2013
Digital ISBN 978-1-61217-675-8

Published in the United States of America

Dedication

To my husband, Mike,
for believing I could do this.
You are my Happy Ever After.

Chapter One

The massive, humpbacked grizzly threw its black snout in the air and snuffled loudly. It rocked back and forth on its powerful forelegs, pushed itself up to a menacing two-legged stance, and raised its huge head.

June Brandt cowered, breathless, flat on her stomach, doing her best to be invisible.

The bear's maw gaped open, and saliva dripped off lips hanging loosely from sharp-edged teeth. Its head swung back and forth, small, thick-lashed eyes half shut, glistening black nose twitching and moist nostrils flaring as it searched for what had disturbed it.

She held her position. The whisper of a breeze poked a long strand of hair into her eye. She didn't dare move to brush it away. A bead of sweat trailed down between her breasts.

The wild silence stretched out intolerably.

Another breath of air raced through the long grasses of the alpine meadow, bringing relief from the heat. The grizzly's distinct scent—an acrid, wildly woolly cologne, salty and dusty—wafted to her. Above the trees edging this high altitude pasture, a hawk wheeled in the currents. Two smaller forms shot out of the tip of a pine, harried the larger bird until it soared out of their space, then returned to their watchtower.

The grizzly dropped to all fours, lowered his head and shook like a dog climbing out of a pond, the thick pelt moving loosely over taut muscles. It was early May, and this large male still had a long way to go to replenish the stores of fat used up surviving last winter. Finally satisfied that what had alarmed him was no threat, he returned to munching dandelions and clover, casually moving away with every scything bite.

When she'd first seen the grizzly in the high mountain field, she'd crept on top of a tumbled pile of boulders at the edge of the trees to get a better look. It was barely four feet high and the scrubby bush surrounding it provided only an illusion of protection. She'd lain there for ages, mesmerized by the majestic animal before her. When she ever so slightly shifted her cramping legs, a small heap of gravel had rattled over the edge, spooking the grizzly.

After a couple of cleansing breaths to settle her pulse, she carefully raised her arms into position. This time, nothing bothered the now placidly chewing bear as she pressed the shutter button on her camera.

She took a number of photos until the huge beast shuffled a safe—well, safer—distance away, then slipped down the far side of the rocky outcrop, bent at the waist and scuttled deeper into the cover of the forest. Without stopping, she tucked her camera into her backpack and continued through the thinning forest as she slung the straps over her shoulders. She pumped uphill, following a narrow track with fewer roots and loose rocks on which to twist an ankle. A couple of minutes later, she broke through the tree line. Several metres further up, she stopped and sat down on a sun-warmed rock.

The spiky tips of the trees through which she had hiked spread out below her. Uncountable shades and hues of green rolled up and down into the distance, blending to purple at the farthest reaches before fading into a soft indigo edge against the sky. Rising away from the curve of the earth, violet lightened to a true sky-blue in which the globe of the sun burned. The air was so clear she could count individual needles on the pines and spruce. Far away, sunlight sparked off water as it struck the silt-laden, swift-flowing Fraser River and glittered off the aluminum roof of a house in the tiny village of Longworth, nestled at the foot of the mountain.

She rose and began toiling uphill once more.

Her feet, cushioned by thick socks inside hiking boots, ached, as did her calves and thighs. Frequent runs while in town kept her in good shape, but nothing prepared muscles for this kind of hike. By the time she reached the relatively flat top of the mountain she was puffing.

Bald mountaintops jutting up above the tree line pierced the green coniferous blanket covering much of the northern half of British Columbia. On strategically chosen peaks, thinly scattered across this enormous landmass, were lookouts where men and women, unafraid of isolation and possessed of great stamina, stood guard during the summer fire season, using eyes and experience to discover and track potentially devastating wildfires. Modern technology had not yet superseded this vital service, but over the years, many of the structures had been abandoned, and were now inhabited only by squirrels, birds and other resourceful creatures. She was headed to one of these deserted structures.

It faintly resembled the top layers of a decrepit

wedding cake. The bottom level was sided with vertical wooden planks, once painted blue, now weathered to a dull grey that camouflaged the tower against the rocks. The door was set in the south side of the building, with square windows on each of the other walls. The slightly smaller upper level, where the equipment would have been mounted during fire spotting days, was walled in glass, with a steeply pitched shingle roof.

June pushed the warped and battered door and propped it open with a stick jammed into the gap on the hinge side. Swinging her pack off her shoulders, she tossed it on the table, unclipped her canteen and poured warm and faintly dusty water down her dry throat. Swiping her mouth with the back of her hand, she sank onto one of two rickety chairs and bent to undo the laces of her hiking boots.

The building was dry and clean, other than the mice and squirrel droppings she'd found in the bare cabinets. In the far corner, a plywood sheet attached to two walls with a four-by-six post supporting the outside edge made a rudimentary bed. It would be plenty comfortable once cushioned by the thin foam pad she'd brought. A small wood stove, where she could cook simple meals, squatted a few feet from the wall, opposite the door, and a trapdoor in the ceiling gave access to the lookout on the roof.

Just outside, a simple gutter system led to an old wooden cask, three-quarters full of rainwater. When she had arrived earlier that day, she had cautiously poked the water with a branch, stirring it up in order to discover any drowned creatures. When none floated to the surface, she had covered the barrel with an old piece of plywood discarded against the side of the shack and weighted it down with a couple of rocks. Padding across the floor in her sock feet, she pushed the makeshift lid off to the side. She rinsed her hands in the cool water, then ran her fingers through the long, blond strands of her hair, casually untangling knots. Removing the bandanna from around her neck, she dipped it into the water and used it to wipe the sweat of fear and exertion from her face, neck, and arms.

A brisk breeze swirled through the doorway. Up this high, there was never really a chance to get too hot. Right now the heat beat down with pleasant strength, but it was an illusion that would vanish quickly when the sun faded below the horizon. She pulled her shirt over her head and let the wind ruffle goose bumps across her midriff and back. Stepping inside, she spread her foam mat and sleeping bag on the plywood bed and lay down in her bra and shorts.

In today's world, finding a place free of mankind's sounds was difficult, if not impossible. Even high on a mountain, she sometimes heard voices from the few homes below, floating up on mysterious drafts of air. The rail line was still in regular use, and the whistles of trains as they glided past Longworth echoed eerily many times throughout the day and night. But right now, all was peace.

She fell asleep.

****

Chuka-chuka-chuka. She woke abruptly, took a moment to register the noise, then stumbled to a window. The helicopter pilot was delicately positioning the small machine a safe distance from the tower. Two fast strides brought her to the table where she had thrown her T-shirt. She pulled it on as she headed for the door. Waiting as the rotor blades whirled slower and slower, she shielded her eyes from the sun as it set stunningly, directly behind the aircraft. All she could see was the outline of the pilot silhouetted inside. He pulled off his headphones, reached up to open the door, and slid out, turning back immediately to lean into the cockpit.

"Hello!" she called over the ticking of the engine and the humming of the blades.

The pilot spun on his heel, ducking adroitly to avoid banging his head on the door frame. "Good Lord!" he choked. "Where'd you come from?"

June made soothing motions with her hands. "Sorry to startle you." She was relieved to see his shoulders relax and the fierce glare he'd given her smooth out. "I was in the lookout. I hiked up earlier. Planning to spend a few days." She pointed with her chin at the helicopter. "Nice ride."

He smiled. The skin crinkling around his rich brown eyes was a shade lighter than the rest of his face, probably caused by wearing the dark sunglasses now tucked into the open neck of his light green shirt. "Yeah, well, I'm here on business." She noticed the emblem on the chest pocket, and therefore wasn't surprised when he introduced himself. "Alex Weaver. Conservation officer, Ministry of the Environment—Fish and Wildlife. I didn't expect anyone to be up here."

"I could tell." She approached the machine, peering curiously through the plexiglass, then offered her hand. "June Brandt. Sorry again."

"Hey, no problem." He released her hand and reached a long arm into the helicopter to pull out a large pack similar to hers. "We had a report of poachers in the area, so I came to check it out. How long have you been here?"

"Since this morning. My truck's parked down in Longworth. I haven't seen anyone all day."

"A couple of hikers phoned it in. They'd seen a bear carcass, maybe a grizzly, somewhere on the north slope. Trouble is they were here last Saturday, and only decided to call today." He shook his head at the delay. Dark brown, almost black, hair fell into his eyes, and he flicked it away with the back of his wrist. "Plus, their directions are kind of vague. They know they followed the main trail up here, and then went over the crest to the other side. Have you been that way?"

"No, not yet." She gestured toward the lookout, and they headed inside. "Once I brought my gear up here, I backtracked a bit down the trail to a meadow on the tree-line." They sat in the shaky chairs. "I saw a grizzly there, but it certainly wasn't dead."

One dark eyebrow rose. "How close were you? See any cubs?"

"Close enough. No cubs. I'm fairly sure it was a male, based on the size of him. Here, I've got photos."

While she dug her camera out of her pack and turned it on, Alex pulled out a water bottle and tilted his head back to take a drink. His neck was darkly tanned, with a hint of paler skin showing at the collar.

"There he is," she said, handing him the camera.

He studied the shots closely, agreed with her assessment of the bear being male, then looked at her oddly. "This camera doesn't have much of a zoom on it." It was a tiny point-and-shoot she found handier to bring camping than the larger, fancier SLR she also owned.

"It doesn't," she said cheerfully.

His eyes narrowed. "Exactly how close were you?"

"I stayed out of sight, and did nothing that would attract him." Nothing on purpose. She pointed out the window, where the sun was descending. "Isn't it kind of late to do any scouting tonight? I would have thought you'd wait until tomorrow."

He shrugged good-naturedly. "It didn't matter whether the helicopter came out this evening or tomorrow morning, so I decided to spend the night. Like I said, I didn't think anyone would be here."

"It's not the kind of place you make a reservation."

He laughed. "I guess not."

The last of the sun's rays streamed in through the western window, glittering with motes of dust. "There's plenty of room on the floor," she offered resignedly, "so you might as well stay. I've got dibs on the bed, such as it is."

Again one dark eyebrow quirked upward. "You sure?"

It was her turn to shrug. "Have you got any ID?" He reached two fingers into the breast pocket of his shirt and fished out a leather wallet. She studied the formal government identification, took one of his business cards and handed back the wallet. "Good enough for me."

She stood up from the table and crossed to the cupboards, where she had stored her cooking gear and food. "I was going to make myself something to eat. Are you hungry?" It might be after nine o'clock but she'd napped through dinner.

"I ate before I left, but I wouldn't say no to a cup of coffee."

Using a minimal amount of paper and kindling, she managed to get the pot-bellied stove going in a reasonably expert fashion. The chimney rose for a couple of feet, then made a right angle and vented through the back wall of the cabin.

Earlier she'd checked it for bird nests and squirrel pantries, so she was fairly certain she wouldn't smoke them out.

She put water on to boil. While it was heating, she assembled her percolator coffee pot, scooping grounds into the metal basket and snapping on the lid, then placing it next to the pan on the stove top.

Alex headed for the door. "I should finish securing the 'copter, make sure it's set for the night." She nodded briefly as she poured pasta into the pot.

Through the small window over the counter she watched him head first to the north edge of the mountaintop. He paused on the brink to scan the valley below.

The main trail from Longworth came up the steep but relatively accessible south side. The north side had a more gradual slope, leading into a deep but wide valley, rising again to more mountainous peaks beyond.

Dusk was lowering, and she knew it would be no use searching for anything tonight. Alex Weaver appeared to come to the same conclusion as he shrugged then strode to his machine.

The door was still open, and the breeze blowing in was noticeably cooler than an hour ago. She mixed shredded cheese in with the pasta, stirred it with her fork, and ate right from the pot. Carrying it with her, she wandered out the door.

Turning away from the helicopter, she found a

convenient spot, and settled down on crossed legs to enjoy the final minutes of the day.

She sighed as she scraped out the last of the macaroni and licked off the fork. She had come to this lonely mountain hoping for some time alone as a way to rejuvenate after a busy year at university. The conservation officer's abrupt appearance had put paid to her solitude, but she consoled herself with the fact that he would probably be leaving the next day.

Catching poachers in the act was practically impossible, and convictions were usually precisely and painstakingly constructed by the careful gathering of evidence. If Alex Weaver found the carcass tomorrow, he'd be gone before nightfall, and she'd be alone as she wished.

She clambered to her feet and paced back to the darkened cabin. Treading through the gloom to her backpack, she pulled out a small, battery-operated lantern, placed it on the counter, and switched it on. It lit the tiny room nicely. The coffee started perking, so she pulled her mug from the cupboard and rustled up a sugar packet. She hoped the pilot had brought his own necessities, as she hadn't brought enough dishware for entertaining. Through the window over the washbasin a dark shape was still moving around the helicopter. She dragged a chair closer to the stove, put her feet on the fender, and sipped her coffee.

The stove was centered to the back wall, about three or four feet into the room, and the remains of the fire gave off a cheering warmth. She leaned her head back to stretch her neck and glimpsed the steel ring of the trapdoor set in the ceiling.

On her feet again, it wasn't much of a stretch for her

to grasp the metal handle. It opened easily, dropping down on its hinges, and a small ladder slid toward her from its resting-place on the door.

Carrying her mug, she stepped up and onto the top floor.

Chapter Two

The sky was a blanket pricked with stars, cuddling the curve of the watery moon, like a mother with her baby in the crook of an arm. It was easy to pick out the constellation all Canadian children learn first, the edge of its ladle pointing the way to the North Star.

The door below shut with a muffled thud, then she heard steady footsteps mounting the ladder. A voice at her ear said, “Amazing, isn’t it.”

Without turning her head, she smiled. “Easy to forget how many stars there are, when you spend too much time in the city.” He stood at her side, his shoulder brushing hers, silently gazing at the cosmos. “Makes me wonder about those people who won’t even discuss the possibility of intelligent life out there.”

He rested on his palms against the window sill, and glanced sideways at her. “You must admit, it’s a very uncomfortable concept. Especially if they find us first.”

“I guess that’s one way to think of it. Me, I wonder what they might be like.”

He turned to her. For a moment the romance of the scene filled her senses: a man, a woman, as alone as Adam and Eve. The scent of pine trees and wildflowers. No sound but the wind. It was not a smart way to feel about a man she’d met scant hours before, even if he did seem safe and sexy and sane. She broke the look and moved away, resting a shoulder against one of the corner posts. A small oblong of light from the lantern in the room below escaped out the window and lay on the ground. Serrated tops of trees were a lighter darkness against the obsidian of the sky. The helicopter cast a metallic gleam as it slept under the moonshine.

She heard a rustle, and turned to see Alex with one foot on the top step of the ladder. “Any more coffee?” he asked.

She nodded. “I don’t have a mug for you, though.”

“Brought my own.” He disappeared gracefully through the opening.

She stayed where she was a little longer, absently tracing the grain in the wood of the window frame with a fingertip. Then she, too, returned to the room below.

He stood with his hips against the counter, cupping a mug in his hands. She lifted the chair she’d put near the stove, carried it across the room, and slid it back underneath the table, then rubbed its chipped, painted shoulders.

He drained his cup, and placed it on the counter. “I figured I’d spread my bag upstairs.”

“You’re more than welcome to the floor down here if you like.”

“I’ll be fine. It’s all set to be a beautiful night.”

“It’s up to you.”

An awkward silence drooped over them, as if, like her, Alex wasn’t sure how to say goodnight. He grabbed his pack-sack. “Guess I’ll head up then. See you in the morning.”

“Sleep well.”

He climbed the treads, reached down, and lifted the door until it clicked into place. His footsteps shuffled quietly for a few minutes, and then all was still.

She snapped off the lantern, leaving the room bathed in pale moonlight. She slipped off her socks, boots and shorts, then slid into her sleeping bag. Crossing her arms behind her head, she relaxed into the snug flannel. The lunar glow flowed through the window near her bed, and she lay awake, enjoying the deep peace. Then, softly, gently, the breathing of the night wind lulled her imperceptibly to sleep.

****

Alex woke early the next morning. His nose was frosty and the air was damp, but the dawn sunlight fell on his cheek with a hint of the heat to come. Last winter, they'd had below average snowfall, and spring had been warmer than normal. Buzz in the office was the forest fire season was going to be frantic.

He certainly hadn't expected to see anyone else on top of the mountain when he'd headed out the day before, but he wasn't bothered by the company. June Brandt's calm and confident air appealed to him, and she seemed well-prepared for a few days away from civilization. He'd been involved in too many search and rescue operations to be lenient toward anyone who didn't take the wilderness seriously. He was glad she wasn't one of those.

During the minutes they'd spent contemplating the night sky he'd been caught unaware by the possibilities swirling in the air between them, and had decided retreat was the better part of valour. He was here to do a job, quickly and efficiently. That didn't stop him from remembering her profile, edged with moonlight: nose a hint too long, sharp chin. Scandinavian, maybe German, heritage, he speculated, especially with all that gorgeous fair hair.

Conscious of June directly beneath him, he rolled up his sleeping mat and bag, raised the trapdoor, and stepped noiselessly down into the room below.

She slept on, peaceful and innocent, curled up on her side with a hand beneath her cheek, bright blond hair scattered about. She breathed deep and even as he slipped past her and out the door to take care of the morning's necessary business, and was still sleeping when he returned.

He did his best to move silently, but couldn't avoid the occasional creak of wood on wood, a mildly reverberating clang as he pulled off the lid of the coffee pot, the snick of a cupboard door opening and closing. June shifted restlessly, long legs twisting in the red and blue sleeping bag. Her eyes opened slowly, a frown creasing her forehead.

"Morning," she said, voice clogged and rough.

"Morning. I was hoping I wouldn't wake you, but..." he gestured with the coffee pot, "...the only thing that makes the dawn worthwhile."

"Dawn?" She sat up and wrapped the sleeping bag around her waist, yawning. "What time is it?"

"Six-thirty."

She groaned. "Nothing like sleeping in when you're on holiday."

"Ah, but I'm not. I want to find that carcass today. It's already been almost a week since the hikers saw it."

Flipping back the sleeping bag, she slid her legs out. Alex caught a glimpse of strong calves and slim thighs as she snagged her shorts from the floor beside the bed, and in one swift motion pulled them on while getting to her feet. She turned to face him, smoothing her hands down the front of her T-shirt as if trying to iron out the wrinkles.

"Will you make enough for me?" She pointed to the coffeepot.

"Already did."

"Be right back, then." Plucking a plastic zip-lock bag from her pack-sack, she headed out the door.

She returned with her hair twisted into a loose bun at the nape of her neck and her face shiny from a cold water wash. A grumpy pout still teased the corners of her mouth. Alex hid a grin as she walked by.

"How do you plan on finding the bear?" she asked as she tucked her bathroom bag away and tidied up her bed.

He poured steaming coffee from the metal pot into two mugs. "I'll follow the directions from those hikers as best I can, and keep my eyes peeled. I should be able to spot ravens or eagles scavenging."

He handed her a mug, and she took a cautious sip. "What'll you do if you find it?"

He pointed to his pack, next to the door, ready to go. "I've got an evidence kit in there: bags, tags, camera. I'll get as much information as I can from the site. Anything might lead us to the people responsible." He ripped open a high-energy protein bar and took a bite. "What are your plans for the day?"

June opened a bag of granola and began to munch. "Footloose and fancy free." She eased onto one of the derelict chairs, propping one foot on the other.

"How well do you know this area?"

"Pretty well." She made a back and forth motion with her hand. "I have an aunt and uncle with a cabin down below, and we used to hike up once in a while when we came to visit. I haven't been here by myself for a couple of years, though."

Any woman assured enough to spend time alone on a remote mountaintop was obviously resourceful and intrepid. Alex found his interest in June growing. He remembered her nonchalant attitude as she told of her encounter with the grizzly, and offered up a challenge. "I could use the extra pair of eyes, if you want to head out with me."

She didn't jump at the chance, but considered it as she chewed. "Sure. Why not?"

They cleared away the breakfast remnants and closed the cabin door, blocking it shut to keep out pests. Alex set a brisk pace as they trudged down the north side of Longworth Mountain.

"The callers said they'd hiked about an hour from the lookout before they discovered the carcass," he said. "It was in a narrow crevasse off to the left of the trail. They didn't examine it too closely, as they'd just noticed the time, and realized they'd have to hurry if they were going to get back down before dark." He hitched his pack into a more comfortable position on his shoulders. "We'll have to keep our eyes open."

On this side of the mountain, it was easy to believe they were the only people for thousands of kilometres. The ever-present breeze sang through the grasses, underscoring the intermittent melody of bird calls, a subtle chorus to the crunch of boots on rocks and the rustle of swinging arms. The track descended at a shallow angle, with the occasional steep section, dodging around large boulders and switching back on itself. They concentrated on the job at hand and there was little chatter. He was pleased June kept up easily, and after about forty-five minutes they were deep in the wide valley. A brilliant sun beamed down on them.

Alex halted, slung his backpack to the ground, unclipped a water bottle and took a long drink. "We should be getting close."

She copied his actions, perching on a rock. "Look."

He followed her gaze further down the valley. Three or four black figures flapped lazily against the polished sky, and a rusty, raucous calling drifted on the increasingly heated air. "Good eye," he said. "Ready?"

"Let's go."

The trail was relatively straight and level, and it wasn't long before the fresh scent of wildflowers, dust and leaves was tainted with the stench of death. A low, growling buzz raised the hair on Alex's neck. He glanced over his shoulder and gestured for June to stay back. She stopped obediently and waited while he stepped toward a cleft in the rock to their left.

He peered in the opening, covering his nose and mouth with the crook of his elbow. The stink was incredible, but the insects were worse. The grizzly's carcass was covered in a moving sheet of glossy black flies, thousands upon thousands of them. Hundreds more hung like fog. Soon they were swarming around him, drawn by salty sweat. He backed away from the opening.

He lowered his arm. "It's going to be ugly," he said. "But if you can stand it, I could certainly use your help."

She moved forward and looked around him into the narrow space. She sucked in a breath, making a slight choking sound when the full force of the decomposing body struck her, but she stood her ground.

She turned to him, her face pale under the light tan of early summer, but she regarded him steadily, her voice matter of fact. "What do we do now?"

He pulled out a small digital camera. "Get some pictures," he said. "First, with the flies." He snapped a few shots of the fissure's entrance, then advanced in, getting various angles. He called back to her, "Let's see what we can do about those flies now. Cut me a couple switches, would you?"

She dug a small blade from one of the many pockets on her shorts, and hacked off a few of the leafiest branches from a nearby willow. Then, armed with those, they headed back into the rocky cleft.

It was a buzzing, foul-smelling hell. Flies shrouded them, blundering drunkenly like tiny, black hailstones. After a few minutes of determined flailing, the worst of the insects were gone, and they could see what remained of the bear.

The glossy dark brown fur had dulled and dimmed in death. The head was missing, leaving a gory stump on which a few persistent flies still gorged. All four paws had been roughly amputated. And it had been disemboweled.

"If you can stand staying with me, keep moving those branches." He handed her the ones he had used. "I'll be as quick as I can."

While she waved the willow boughs to keep most of the flies from returning, he took more pictures. Then he slipped on thin, latex gloves and searched meticulously around the carcass, including the pile of entrails. Despite June's efforts, dozens of insects droned about them, irresistibly drawn to the carnage. The tiny beasts crawled in his hair, on the back of his neck, up the cuffs of his sleeves, but he ignored them and calmly continued his inspection.

His search spread in ever widening circles, until he finally nodded and motioned to the opening. June backed out, relief evident on her face.

He stripped off the bloody gloves. “Thanks.” He scrubbed his hands through his hair, scattering flies.

She swished off a few insects lingering on his shoulders and back. “Are they usually this bad?” she asked as they retreated farther away from the crevasse.

“The flies? It depends when you find the body, and where. It didn’t help, tucking the carcass into that narrow space.”

“Tucking it? You mean the bear wasn’t shot there?”

“Dirt was piled up against the shoulders, as if it had been pushed or pulled in. Which means more than one poacher for sure. There’s no way a single person shifted that bear. It had to be close to three hundred pounds.”

“Did you find anything else?”

“You saw the obvious bits. And the gall bladder was missing. Other than that, not a damn thing.” He paused in rearranging his equipment and sat back on his heels.

“Will you catch them?”

“It’s not very likely.” He puffed out a breath. It probably wouldn’t have made any difference, but the nearly one week delay in getting to the kill site frustrated him. “Not from any evidence here.”

Now they were at a distance from the remains of the bear, fresh, alive scents like warm dust and peppery wildflowers filled the air. A movement on the far side of the valley caught his eye—a rabbit, hopping out from under a bush to nibble on succulent new grass. As soon as it came to rest, he lost sight of it, expertly camouflaged in its mottled brown coat.

"Is it really worth it?" she wondered. "For the poachers, I mean? Or is it just for the thrill?"

He laughed shortly. "Worth it? Almost no risk, and extremely high returns. Do you know why they take the gallbladder?"

"It's used in traditional Chinese medicine."

"They believe bear bile is a cure-all. It's been used for thousands of years. And do you know how much buyers will pay?"

She shook her head.

"Each gall bladder can net a poacher up to ten thousand dollars. Ten thousand! Per gram, that's more lucrative than cocaine. The paws are used for soup. It's supposed to cure respiratory and gastrointestinal problems. In Asian restaurants in the US, you can buy a bowl of bear paw soup for about sixty dollars. Overseas, a bowl can cost as much as one thousand dollars US."

She stared at him. "I knew bear parts were valuable, but I had no idea that much money was involved."

"Most people don't. Poaching rarely makes the big city newscasts, and even when we do manage to catch someone, the fines are so small they don't even warrant coverage. It is possible for poachers to be sentenced jail time, but…" His shoulders jerked. "Canada has the largest wild black bear population remaining in the world. China has topped one billion people, and that doesn't include the rest of the Asian world, where traditional Chinese medicine is just as popular. You figure it out." He stood abruptly, slipped his arms through the straps of his pack and jiggled it into position. "We should head back. Ready?"

She tilted her head, eyes thoughtful, and they began their return.

They were scrambling up a particularly steep section of the path when the shot rang out. Alex, a few feet below June on the slope, snagged her wrist and yanked her to the ground. “Where the hell did that come from?”

Another shot boomed through the still, mountain air. She pointed to a bright flash on the opposite side of the valley. “There. Close to that big crack in the far wall.” The glint of sunlight reflected off a recoiling rifle barrel.

“Stay here,” Alex said, then was off, racing down the slope.

Chapter Three

He heard footsteps and risked a glance behind. June hustled after him, a determined look on her face. He opened his mouth to shout at her to get back, but she yelled, "Don't even bother," as she dodged a low thicket.

They dashed across the valley floor, weaving around boulders and brush shoulder to shoulder. The fissure in the mountain wall grew as they neared it. Dropping to a walk, he scanned the wall, checking left and right. "Nothing. Maybe he went in." He forged into the gully. The floor was strewn with large rocks, hummocks of grass, and small, wiry shrubs, and barely wide enough for the two of them to walk side by side.

"What are we doing?" she hissed.

"Seeing what we can see." He kept moving, picking his way carefully forward.

"There's no one here."

"Keep searching. There can't be too many places to hide."

They followed the ravine deep into the mountain, until the sky was a bright blue gash in the air high above them and they reached a vertical wall a mountain goat would have trouble scaling.

Nothing.

She slung off her pack, slumped against the rock wall and slid to the ground. Sweat beaded her forehead and ran from her temples. He followed suit, feeling the dampness of his own shirt against his back as he leaned against the sun-heated stone.

"I don't know," she said. "I guess whoever it was didn't come in here." She took a long drink from her bottle, the muscles in her slender throat flexing.

"It was only a chance. And a slim one at that." His own water was stale and tasteless, but a welcome relief. "Chasing them was probably a lost cause, but we might have caught them if they ducked in here. Maybe they knew it was a dead end."

He dribbled a small amount of water over his head, letting it run down the back of his neck, then poured the tepid liquid into June's cupped hands. She splashed her face and used the hem of her T-shirt as a towel. He caught a glimpse of flat stomach muscles and a small, round dark mole beside her navel. Relaxing back, he gazed up into the narrow slice of cloudless sky framed above the gully's edge.

She propped her elbows on her bent knees. "Do you think that was the poacher? And was he aiming at us?"

He took another sip from his flask. "I don't know. But poachers aren't murderers. They certainly wouldn't want to draw attention to themselves by attacking a human near a recent kill. And unless they've been watching us for a long time, they'd have no reason to suspect we're anyone other than casual hikers." He shrugged angrily. "This place is perfect for poachers—reasonably accessible yet remote, and teeming with both blacks and grizzlies. If the hunter that killed our bear is feeling lucky, he might be back."

She rose, hefted her pack to her shoulders and reached out. He gripped her hand, feeling the slight roughness that spoke of outdoor work, and let her help him to his feet.

"Let's try this again," she said, "and see if we make it all the way back this time."

They made the return trip at a much less breakneck pace. "We haven't really had a lot of trouble with bear poachers recently," he said. "It's mostly ungulates, like deer, elk and moose. And a lot of the time it's simply a trigger-happy hunter who shot the wrong animal—big bull without a tag, or cow moose out of season. If our dead grizzly and whoever was shooting now are connected, then I'm afraid we might be into something bigger than usual."

"What do you mean?"

"Potentially, a poaching ring. A highly organized group out to make the most of the black market." They reached the other side of the valley and started their climb to the tower. "When are you heading back to town?"

"Couple of days. Why?"

Alex was leading, and when he stopped, she tipped her head back, squinting slightly as the bright, late morning sun shone in her eyes.

"Be careful," he said.

She answered him seriously. "I always am."

Strands of her hair, darkened with sweat, clung to her temples and behind her ears, and her face glowed with exertion. The tug of attraction he'd felt last night gave another yank. "Be extra careful," he repeated. "Please."

They made the rest of the ascent in silence. At the summit, he headed straight for the helicopter, opening the bubble glass door and tossing his pack in. "I should be getting back."

She nodded. "Have you got everything?"

"Packed it all this morning before you were up." He smiled. "You do sleep soundly."

She made a face, turning down the corners of her wide mouth. "As long as I wasn't drooling."

He circled the helicopter, readying it for flight, then lifted himself into the cockpit, leaving the door open for the moment. "Thanks for your help today. I know it was gruesome, but it's important." She nodded, and he added, "You should stop by the office when you get back to town."

"Do you want me to give a report of what happened?"

"That wouldn't hurt, but I was thinking you might enjoy meeting some of the other people around the place, take a look around." He had been extremely impressed with her composure at the kill site, and even more so with her poise during and after the gunshots. She stood before him, not classically beautiful but long-limbed, athletic and dynamic. "Also, I wouldn't mind seeing you again, for myself."

She considered him, a glint in her eyes. "I don't think I'd mind seeing you again, for myself. Maybe I will."

"Think about it." He shut the door and reached up to lock it in place. She backed away to the cabin, and waited the few minutes it took him to go through the pre-flight checks. The engine pitch rose to a whine as the rotors reached the correct speed, and then he was off, like a clumsy dragonfly lifting from a reed. Hovering, he caught a last glimpse of her, defiantly alone in the vast wilderness, then headed back to civilization.

****

"There you are!" A tall woman with a braided rope of red hair stood up and beckoned to June as she walked through the doorway. "Come, sit over here!"

Weaving her way through the ranks of chairs, June sat down next to her. The woman leaned in closer. "I'm so glad you came," she said confidentially. "Now you're here we can poke fun at Thomas."

June had arrived back in town that afternoon. After a long, luxurious shower, she'd headed right back out again, in time for this meeting held at the University of Northern British Columbia, a small, young institution stretching its wings from its perch on the hills above Prince George.

About a dozen men and women were spread about the room. One lanky woman wearing a Sherpa-style toque was pinning an anti-poaching poster to the bulletin board. On the whiteboard at the front of the room the title "RiverForce" headed a list of agenda items. A pudgy young man, oddly dressed in a collared shirt and tie paired with khaki walking shorts, fidgeted with papers on the podium. He smoothed back his fine, blond hair awkwardly, using his wrists instead of his palms.

"We will not poke fun at anyone," June scolded with a laugh in her voice. "Thomas is doing his best, and we shouldn't tease him."

"Oh, pooh." Tabitha Scala waved off that sentiment with one long-fingered, be-ringed hand.

"I thought Richard was coming."

"Of course he is," Tabitha said. "Why else would I be here? But Thomas said Richard warned he might be late, so we're stuck with Tubby Tom, at least for a bit." She was dressed in her usual costume of long, flowing caftan and open-toed canvas sandals, with a colourful headscarf tied at her nape and streaming down her back. Multitudinous beaded necklaces twined around her slender neck and dozens of narrow silver bracelets clinked and tinkled on her thin wrists.

Thomas knocked sharply on the rostrum's wooden surface. "All right, everyone. If you could please take a seat, we'll get going."

It was a sparse crowd, and three times as many chairs had been set out as were needed. It would have been better, June mused, to have put out too few chairs and bring in more only if necessary.

RiverForce Environmental Group consisted mostly of undergrads in the Natural Resource program and a few concerned residents such as Tabitha. June had joined a couple of years ago, and it hadn't taken her long to see that the group suffered from good intentions without a strong guiding focus. The main goal—if the group had such a thing—was to alert residents to the signs of poaching, and to let them know what to do if they discovered such evidence. Most of the members' time was spent at various trade shows and exhibitions, manning information booths.

All that was changing now.

Thomas requested volunteers to make a motion and to second the agenda. Two hands were lackadaisically raised, and he noted the names. Tabitha whispered caustic comments in June's ear as he reviewed the minutes from the last meeting. People shifted on their chairs restlessly.

The door flung open, and Richard Fleetham marched into the room.

"Oh, goody," sighed Tabitha.

"Hello, everyone! Sorry I'm late." Richard walked briskly down the centre aisle and slapped Thomas on the shoulder. "Where are we?"

Everyone sat up straighter. The entire room seemed to fill with fresh air and crackling energy.

A new instructor at the university, Richard Fleetham had become faculty advisor to RiverForce, and was breathing new life into its well-meaning corpse. It wasn't only his vigorous speech that enlivened the group. Everything about him seemed coiled and ready. He was constantly moving—snapping his fingers, tapping his feet. Even his thick black hair, tightly curled and springy, seemed infused with vitality. He often scrubbed his fingers through it as though combing ideas and thoughts out of his brain. Bushy eyebrows grew forcefully above snapping green eyes, and he sported a luxuriant beard he kept ruthlessly trimmed into a smart goatee.

"We were beginning to discuss the government's new hunting regulations." Thomas stepped deferentially away from the podium.

"Excellent, excellent." Richard clapped his hands together delightedly.

He had a way of using just the right tone and words to inspire his listeners. And while he preached strongly against poaching and other, more controversial issues, he never appeared militant or fanatical. He was always willing to hear the other side of the story, and usually found a way to diffuse any contentious situation. He'd only moved to the community a few months ago, yet was recognized often on the street due to his appearances on local media. RiverForce had received more publicity since Richard had come along than in all the years before.

"Thanks very much for handling things until I could get here." Richard patted Thomas again and the younger man preened. "Why don't you have a seat and I'll carry on."

With Richard at the helm, the meeting zapped along. Even dry government red tape had redeeming points of interest when he was presenting it. Tabitha actually paid attention and made reasonable suggestions, instead of muttering sarcastic comments. In little more than an hour all the necessary business was finished, and people began to straggle out.

"Come with me." Tabitha grabbed June's wrist and made it impossible for her to do anything but. "I want to talk to Richard."

"Of course you do," June mumbled under her breath. If everyone else had been energized by Richard's leadership, Tabitha had been absolutely galvanized. Unfortunately, it wasn't necessarily because of his dedication to the cause.

"June! Tabitha! How are you?" Richard greeted them.

Tabitha released her hold on June and laid her hand on his arm. "We wanted to say how much we enjoyed tonight's meeting."

"Glad to hear it." He gathered up the loose pages littering the top of the podium. "It's great to work with such a devoted group of people."

"We missed you at the Natural Resources Expo." Tabitha pouted slightly. "I wish you could have been there."

"Yes, sorry about that, but you know I had a conference in Vancouver. It's very important we work with all levels of government, help them understand our needs and priorities here in the North." He turned to the whiteboard, picked up an eraser and started wiping away his notes. "How did it go?"

"It was fantastic. Lots of people stopped to chat. In fact, we ran out of brochures. Rachelle and I managed between us, even though June bailed on us." She shot June an impish look.

"I did not bail on you," she couldn't help exclaiming in self defence. "I never once said I would help out that day. You know I'd planned to go to Longworth then."

"Longworth?" Richard said absently, tucking papers into a folder. "What were you doing there?"

"I took a few days to hike around. Actually, it turned out to be kind of interesting. I met a conservation officer and helped him find the carcass of a poached grizzly."

"No!" Tabitha said, distracted from Richard at last. "What happened?"

June told them about her adventures. Tabitha's eyes widened. When June mentioned the shots she'd heard, Richard banged his knuckles on the metal shelf of the whiteboard and dropped the eraser. His horrified gaze never left her face.

"I have to say, chasing after someone with a rifle is certainly...intrepid," he said, rubbing his hand, "but, really, I can't encourage a repeat of it. You know we are mainly a public relations organization. You should leave the catching of criminals to the experts."

"Don't worry," she said. "I don't think I'll have the opportunity to make it a habit. I do have to say, seeing that poor animal made me realize how important our work is." She shrugged off the dismal memory. "Although some good might come of it. Alex invited me to his office to have a tour, meet some people. Maybe I'll have a foot in the door when it's time to find work after graduation."

"You take care of yourself, sweetie," Tabitha said. "We wouldn't want anything to happen to you."

"No," Richard said as he bent to pick up the eraser, "we wouldn't want that at all."

The setting sun stretched out shadows to impossible lengths as June and Tabitha walked toward the older woman's vintage Volkswagen and said their goodbyes. June had to grin as the battered Beetle swung out on the one-way ring road circling the university, Tabitha's arm waving out the window, beads and bangles glittering.

Her own, not quite so ancient, little red pickup was parked all by itself three rows away. The parking lot had been about two-thirds full when she arrived, but at this time on a Sunday evening only those suffering from a surfeit of desperation or dedication were still here, and vehicles were now few and far between.

She dug in the capacious bag she used as a purse, conducting the usual frustrating search for her keys. It wasn't until the motorcycle was within striking distance that she realized her danger. Moments later, the outstretched arm of the black visored rider struck her fiercely on the side of the head and knocked her spinning, scraping, twisting to the rough pavement.

Chapter Four

Stunned, she sprawled on her stomach on the gritty ground. The vibrations of the machine washed through her body, and dynamic oily swirls danced behind her eyelids. Painfully she opened her eyes. The sun blazed blindingly into them, silhouetting the geometric outlines of the buildings. The glare dimmed as the motorcycle rolled between her and the setting sun. She heard the crunch of its tires and felt the heat of its engine. Fear of robbery, of rape, forced her to her knees, ready for flight. The rumble of the idling engine increased to a roar, and the bike took off in a rush.

The noise of its escape faded away. Tiny pebbles dislodged themselves from her cheek as she crouched, head hanging.

Her bag had been knocked from her arm when she'd spun to the ground, and its contents were scattered everywhere. Her keys lay mockingly close at hand, glittering in the last rays of the sun.

A steady, buzzing tone reverberated in her brain. She crawled gingerly, gathering her belongings, carrying her aching head cautiously on her shoulders. A bruise stiffened her hip, and various scratches and gouges complained loudly.

She pulled herself into the driver's seat, then delicately lowered her head to the steering wheel. Nausea welled up, burning the back of her throat and into her sinuses. She briefly considered calling for help. Oddly enough, Alex was the first person who came to mind. Breathing deeply and evenly, she quelled the worst of her symptoms, then put the truck in gear, and drove home.

****

"You say this rider was aiming for you specifically?"

"He had to be. There was no one else in the lot, hardly any vehicles at all."

It was Monday morning, and June had presented herself at the local RCMP detachment after considerable internal argument. She'd woken up feeling reasonably well and debating the need to cause a fuss. But she couldn't ignore the deliberateness of the attack, and decided it would be best to make an official report.

"You keep saying 'he.' Do you have any reason for that?"

"Not really. I didn't get a good look at all." An image flashed into her mind. "His boots. He was wearing those heavy motorcycle boots, and his feet were really big. I was nose to nose with them for a second, before he raced away." She shrugged. "Sorry I can't be more helpful."

The skin on her forehead was tight, a result of the large goose egg rising there, and she had a stinging three-inch scrape along her jaw bone. Constable Wendy Hoffarth made meticulous notes on her injuries, and even snapped a number of photos. The officer had dark blond hair shorn close to her head, a compact build, and a brusque manner.

"And you can't think of anyone who would have a reason to do this?" Stern blue eyes stared at June.

"Look," she said. "I wanted to get this on file so there's a record of it. But I'm sure it was a random wing-nut. I was the only person in the lot at the time. Someone must have done it for kicks."

Hoffarth studied her awhile longer, then relaxed into her chair. "There was no robbery, and no attack after the first blow, which seems very odd. You didn't get even part of the license plate?"

June shook her head, carefully, as a hint of headache still lingered.

"If anything else happens, be sure to update us." Hoffarth closed her notebook. "And meanwhile, I'll get the information, such as it is, into the system."

"Thanks a lot," June said. "And if I go missing, do search for me, won't you?"

"We're here to help." Hoffarth answered the sarcasm cheerfully. "Seriously, we'll do what we can. And make sure you let us know about anything out of the ordinary."

****

Alex sat in his office, swivelling his chair back and forth, scowling at the photos spread across his desk. His space was standard government-issue, ten feet by ten feet, walls painted dark beige, dusty horizontal blinds hanging on a narrow window with a view of the parking lot. A battered black filing cabinet was tucked in the corner, a large map of Northern British Columbia filled most of one wall, and a well-used whiteboard another.

The photos were ones he'd taken at the poaching scene on Longworth Mountain. He'd studied them often over the last few days, but saw nothing useful. With a low growl of frustration he gathered them up and stuffed them in a file. His phone rang.

"Alex Weaver speaking."

"Hi, Alex. It's June Brandt calling."

"Hey, how are you?" He'd also spent a fair bit of his time over the last few days thinking of June, wondering if she would call, wondering how he might be able to track her down if she didn't. "How was the rest of your time on the mountain?"

"Fine, thank you." Her voice was brisk and bright. "I thought I'd take you up on your offer to come visit the office. Before you forgot you made it."

"I wouldn't have forgotten. Right now?"

"I can be there in five minutes."

He straightened a stack of folders, tossed a couple of pens into a drawer and swept the rest of the tidy office with a critical eye. When the front desk called, he headed down the hall to meet June in reception.

She was studying a poster on the wall, cool and casual in a dark blue scooped neck top with no sleeves and well-fitting jeans. Attraction jolted deep in his gut.

She turned to greet him and he started. A purplish lump marred her forehead and a rough, red scrape stained her pale cheek.

He moved swiftly to her side. "What happened to you?" She flinched as his fingers skimmed over the swelling.

The corner of her mouth quirked. "I was in a bit of an accident yesterday."

He took her chin in the tips of his fingers, turning her head to inspect the damage. "I'd say so." His hand dropped to her waist to shepherd her through the doorway. "You can tell me all about it in my office."

He directed her to a chair and hunkered down next to her, taking her hands in his.

"Was it a car accident?"

"I guess you could say so."

Her hands were cold. He brushed his thumbs lightly across her knuckles as he listened. It was impossible to ignore the vicious bruise on her temple, and the clouds of distress in her eyes, but he did his best to tamp down the anger they kindled.

"I don't get it." She tried to disguise a catch in her voice with a cough, but he heard the quaver. "Why would anyone want to take me out like that? They didn't steal my wallet or my truck, nothing. And it's not like anyone else was around to scare them away. They just knocked me down and left."

He gave her hands a comforting squeeze and stood up. "Want some coffee? Water?"

"Coffee would be great."

"I'll be right back."

When he returned, she accepted the mug and took a sip, shuddering as she absorbed the industrial strength liquid. "Maybe I should have had the water," she said, sounding more like the confident, composed young woman he'd met on the mountain.

"You were at a RiverForce meeting?" She seemed steady enough, so Alex settled behind his desk. "I know about them. An environmental group, right?"

"Yes, sponsored by the university. The faculty advisor is Richard Fleetham. You might have seen him around. He's often in the paper or on the TV news when they need an expert."

"You're interested in environmentalism?"

"I'm in the Natural Resource Management program at the university." He raised an eyebrow and she answered the unspoken question. "Hence my interest in getting my foot in your door, so to speak. Graduation is still a year away, but I guess it's time I decided what I wanted to do. I really enjoyed tagging along with you, and it got me thinking. I also have to admit to a strong sense of curiosity as to how the investigation is going."

"You haven't missed much. I logged all the evidence, made a report of the shooting, and that's where it sits." His frustration must have escaped despite the calm words. She gave him a sympathetic look.

"It must be difficult, with so little to work with."

He scrubbed his hand on the back of his neck. "You better believe it. But we'll keep plugging away." He gestured at her cup. "If you're done, we can take a tour through the building, see who's around."

She took one more sip, then placed the nearly full cup on his desk. He couldn't blame her. The coffee was truly awful.

He led her down a hallway off which stemmed numerous offices almost identical to his own, before knocking on the frame of an open door at the far end.

"Iain, I'm glad you're here. Do you have a minute?"

"Come on in."

"June, this is Iain Prevost, one of our senior conservation officers." Alex ushered her into the office as Iain rose from his chair, revealing a build well over six feet, and skinny with it. He stretched out a hand invitingly, his smile revealing one front incisor slightly crossed over the tooth next to it.

"Ah, so this is the young lady who helped with the kill up by Longworth."

They sat in a couple of battered metal chairs in front of his desk, and Iain lounged in the high-backed office chair behind it, putting his feet up on an open drawer.

"I don't know how much I helped," she said. "And I certainly don't know how much good it will have done. Alex tells me you don't have high hopes for finding whoever did it."

"We do what we can," Iain said simply. "It's our job, and simply because results take time and don't come easy doesn't mean we shouldn't try. To paraphrase a great mind...we must attempt arduous tasks, for there is no worth in that which is not a difficult achievement." He slid a sly glance at Alex.

"For Pete's sake," Alex said. "You know I've got no idea."

"Ovid," Iain said a trifle smugly. "Didn't teach you that in your western university, did they?"

"Iain went to Saint Francis Xavier University," Alex told June, "and along the way picked up an inexhaustible supply of obscure quotes, with which he torments me."

"You're calling one of the master poets of Latin literature obscure?" Iain said in mock amazement. He turned to June. "So, what do you think?"

"About Ovid?" she said demurely.

Iain's eyes sparked with enjoyment. "Another smart-aleck, I see. About our Ministry here. What's your interest?"

Alex listened as Iain and June discussed her studies. Iain was an excellent investigator, and skilled at interviewing. He put June through her paces, but she held her own.

As they stood to leave, Iain came around his desk, cuffing Alex on the shoulder while offering June an approving nod. "It was nice meeting you. Like I said, we can't promise anything, but it wouldn't hurt for you to keep in touch."

Her face lit up. "I appreciate it. Thanks."

Alex toured her through the radio room, evidence locker, and the rest of the complex, ending up back in reception.

She held out her hand. "Thanks so much. I appreciate you taking the time when you must have other things you should be seeing to."

He took her hand, but didn't let go right away. "It occurs to me you've had an exciting few days. First the shooting on Longworth Mountain, then this motorcycle attack."

She laughed. "You know the old saying about things happening in threes. Here's hoping it's not true in this case."

Despite her assurances an escort was unnecessary, he walked her to her truck. As she turned the key in the door lock, he put his hand on her arm. "What are you doing tonight?" Her pulse jumped, the sensitive skin on the inside of her wrist warm and silky under his fingertips. Her high cheekbones stood out sharp and strong in the bright noon light.

"Nothing much."

"Would you like to have dinner with me?"

She hesitated. "I suppose."

He grinned at her wariness. "That sounds positive."

"Yes," she said firmly. "I would like to have dinner with you."

"I'll pick you up at eight."

****

June took a deep breath and opened the door. Alex stood on the small porch, dressed in neatly pressed black trousers and a crisp white shirt that emphasized his tan.

Dark brown eyes widened in appreciation as his gaze travelled over her. She ordered herself not to fidget.

"Wow. You clean up good."

"You didn't say where we were going." She smoothed her hands down her hips self-consciously. "I wasn't sure what I should wear."

She'd washed her hair and let it dry naturally. It waved freely past her shoulders, with long bangs pulled over the bruise on her forehead. After much anxious internal debate she had slipped into a sleek, cherry-red sleeveless blouse with a deep cowl neck, A-line black skirt, and strappy red sandals.

"Let me rephrase." Before she could skitter backward he lifted the hair off her face, studying the damage once more. His lips tightened but his voice remained casual. "You look wonderful."

Heat crept up her neck to her cheeks. "Except for the goose egg and road rash."

"I mean it." His stare was intent. "You are bewitching."

She dropped her eyes, flustered, and stepped back from the doorway. "Would you like to come in? We could have a drink before we go."

"That sounds fine."

Honey sunshine slanting in the big bow window glowed on the slatted wood floor and brightened the orange petals of the gerbera daisies set on the coffee table. Large, bright-patterned cushions were scattered about the room.

Alex relaxed onto the low couch. June felt oddly breathless, having him in her home. "I have wine, beer, iced tea...?"

"Wine would be great."

She went to the kitchen to fetch the bottle of white chilling in the fridge. The two matching wine glasses she owned were washed and ready, waiting on a tray. She carried everything through to the living room and placed it on the coffee table, then lowered herself onto a scarlet and emerald floor pillow.

"This is a beautiful neighbourhood," Alex said as she wielded the corkscrew. "I love these old character homes. Have you lived here long?"

"All my life." She eased the cork out and poured the wine. "This is where I grew up. My parents still own it, but a few years ago they built themselves a new house outside of town. Now I rent from them."

"Do you have a large family?"

She handed Alex his glass. "For these days, I suppose so. Four brothers, no sisters. Sometimes I wonder how we all squeezed into this little place, but we did. I'm second youngest. My baby brother still lives at home, the brother just older than me is at university in Vancouver, the second oldest is in Calgary. My oldest brother lives here in town. He's married and has a son."

He whistled. "You're an auntie?"

"And loving every minute of it." Her lips curved, thinking of her rambunctious toddler nephew. "How about you?"

"Spoiled only child of divorced parents." He shrugged. "I'm used to getting my own way, so watch out."

"And I'm used to fighting for what I want, so that should make us even. If I was your sister, you'd know that."

"But you're not my sister." Alex said with a mischievous glint. "Isn't that lucky."

She swallowed and ran her tongue over suddenly dry lips. The gleam in his eye raised all the tiny hairs on her arms and sent tickling, teasing tendrils flickering through her belly. She finished her wine with a gulp. "Should we be going?"

Alex stood and put out his hand. "Sure," he said. "I'm starving." He pulled her up in one swift motion, circled her waist with his free arm, and drew her close. Standing in her heels, they were much the same height. Bodies barely touching, they stood still. He softly kissed her bruised forehead, trailing his lips down her cheek to rub them gently against the mark on her chin. Icy hot feathers tickled down her spine.

"Better?" he whispered.

"Much," she whispered back.

Alex took her to an elegant restaurant in a renovated heritage house overlooking the Fraser River. Public areas had been restored to honour the original 1920's fashion. The rooms were small, with three or four intimate tables in each. They were seated in a window nook with a sweeping vista of the silt laden river flowing below and the sandy cutbanks stretching above.

There were few other diners. The maître d', a middle-aged man with a complacent paunch and a paucity of hair, brought their drinks and took their meal orders. After he left they sat in a comfortable silence. June gazed contentedly out the window at the rush of water streaming past. When she turned back Alex was studying her yet again.

She lifted an eyebrow. "What?"

He tilted his head to the side. "Nothing. I like looking at you."

Self-consciously she lifted a hand to her forehead.

"Even though I appear to have been dragged over the pavement?" she said. "Oh, wait, I was."

Her attempt at nonchalance didn't lighten Alex's stare. "Even though," he said.

She couldn't hold his look any longer, and let her attention wander to the maître d', ushering other diners to a table in the far corner. With a start she recognized one of the newcomers, and leaned forward to speak without being overheard. "See that man over there, the one with the curly dark hair and the goatee?"

Alex's eyes slipped casually across the room.

"That's Richard Fleetham, from RiverForce," she said.

"Who's with him?"

"I don't know."

The other man was large and bulky, with an impression of strength, not fat. His hair was dark grey and combed aggressively back from a high forehead. His voice rumbled, heavy with an Eastern European, perhaps German, accent, when he spoke to the maître d'. Richard scanned the room casually. He saw June and his hand froze in mid-air as he accepted the menu.

He excused himself from his companion and crossed to their table. "June! Whatever happened?"

"It's just a few scratches and bruises. Alex, I'd like you to meet Richard Fleetham. Richard, Alex Weaver."

Richard absently shook hands. "But, really, tell me what happened to your lovely face."

"I had a bit of an accident after the meeting last night," she said. "A motorcyclist knocked me down."

His brows narrowed in concern. "Did he not see you?"

"It was so quick. I'm not really sure how it

happened."

Richard understood what she wasn't saying. "You mean it was on purpose. Why on earth would someone do that to you? Did he take anything?"

"Nothing. It's all a bit of a mystery."

"I should say so. I'm certainly glad to see you're okay. We wouldn't want to lose you from our RiverForce team." He glanced over to where a waiter was now presenting a bottle of wine to the heavyset man. "I must get back to my guest. It was a pleasure to meet you, Alex."

He started toward his table, then paused. "You wouldn't be the same Alex that June was telling me about yesterday? The conservation officer she assisted?"

"I am," Alex said.

"Any news on the investigation?"

"Unfortunately not."

"It's an awful situation." Richard shook his head. "I wish you luck catching the criminals."

June watched him take his seat. He spoke quietly to the other man, who turned his head toward her. His eyes were a hard, pale blue, and an odd sense of disquiet crept across her shoulders as he surveyed her dourly. Then her view was blocked by the waiter, weaving through the tables with a plate in each hand, fingers protected with large, snowy white napkins, and she shook off her uneasiness.

She and Alex dined on rare roast beef, fresh asparagus, and baked potatoes, and enjoyed a leisurely, exploratory conversation. They were sharing a decadently sweet piece of chocolate cake when Richard and his foreign-sounding guest left. Richard nodded affably from across the room, but his companion remained austere and aloof, ignoring June when she responded to the salute.

As they waited for the cheque, June reached across and ran a finger over Alex's knuckles as his hand rested darkly against the brilliant white linen. He met her eyes and she was dazzled by a sudden surge of attraction.

She made sure her voice was cool and friendly. "Thanks for a lovely meal."

"Thanks for sharing it with me."

He drove her home in his drab olive green Jeep. Its black hard top, sturdy frame and four wheel drive suited his personality perfectly—dependable, but ruggedly sexy.

He pulled up to the curb in front of her house. A streetlight behind him lit his profile sharply, accenting the strong lines of his face.

She wondered, ill at ease, what the next step should be. "Thanks again for dinner."

"No problem."

He reached across and sleeked a finger down her bare arm, grasping her hand where it lay loosely in her lap. He raised it to his mouth, brushing his lips over her palm, his eyes never leaving her face. "Good night, June."

She heard herself say, "Do you want to come in? I mean, for coffee, or another drink, or something."

His scrutiny was a physical thing, weighting down her limbs, pounding through her blood. "Oh, I'd like to come in for...something," he said, a shameless glimmer in his eye. "But not tonight, I think."

Disappointed, but also a teensy bit relieved, she sighed. "That's probably best."

She tugged her hand from his grip and slid out of

the Jeep with her best attempt at gracefulness. He drove off, a small smile on his lips.

She backed cautiously away from the curb, as if she had been standing on the high diving board, and had decided to climb off the ladder at the last second.

Chapter Five

June had no chance to see Alex during the next few days. Although her heaviest workload of classes was done for the year, she was picking up credits by taking part in a summer session program that ran for five days straight. She spent a lot of the time at various field locations, studying the practices of forest management in regards to water resources. When all necessary reading and homework assignments were added to the hours on-site, she had very little free time. But five concentrated days gained her the same number of credits as a semester long lecture course, with the added bonus of being able to spend most of it outdoors.

The sunny weather she'd enjoyed while on Longworth Mountain held through the week, but Saturday night thunderheads rolled in, bringing high winds and slashing rain. By Sunday morning the worst of it had blown over. She stood sipping her coffee and peering at her backyard through a water pebbled window. Yesterday a few stubborn blossoms still clung to the old apple tree in the corner. Today the pink and white petals were scattered across the lawn.

The phone rang and she answered it with a cheerful hello.

"Hey," Alex said. "How'd your course go?"

"Excellent." She savoured the warmth curling low inside her at the sound of his voice. They'd managed to exchange a few brief text messages since the evening they'd spent together, and she was mildly surprised at how much she'd missed speaking with him. "How was your week?"

"Uneventful until late yesterday. I was on call, and we got a tip. Another grizzly."

"Where?"

"McGregor area. A tree planting crew found it. I'm heading out right away. Want to come along?"

"Are you sure?"

"I'm taking the 'copter. I can pick you up on my way to the airport."

"I'll be ready."

She packed her small rucksack with bottled water, granola bars, extra socks, and a polar fleece. Then she dressed in heavy cotton pants and short sleeved T-shirt under a light wind breaker. Pulling on thick socks, she thrust her feet into sturdy hiking boots. She was waiting on the sidewalk when Alex drove up. He unlocked the door, and she hopped in.

He was wearing his uniform, and looked sexily official, especially with the aviator glasses hiding his eyes. "So, where exactly are we going?" she asked.

"The supervisor of a tree planting crew gave me the coordinates from his GPS. This carcass was found about three miles from the other, as the crow flies." He changed lanes to pass a lumbering motor-home with Texas plates. They crossed the Yellowhead Bridge over the Fraser River.

"Could it be the same poacher?"

"It's certainly possible."

When they arrived at the airport, Alex parked next to a yellow, metal sided building. He unlocked the padlock securing a gate in the chain-link fence, and they carried their bags to the helicopter sitting on the tarmac.

"You can stow your stuff in here." He opened a small panel and moved aside to let her slide her pack in. "You can get in the other side while I do my checks."

The dash was a maze of instruments, some of which seemed fairly straightforward, others whose function she couldn't even guess at. A headset hung on a hook by her head. She put it on and adjusted the fit. Alex swung into the pilot's seat, put on his headset, flicked switches, and twiddled knobs. The rotors started to spin, gradually picking up speed. Vibrations hummed through the hull.

After receiving permission from the tower, Alex began manipulating the two hand levers. The helicopter broke away from the ground with a small jerk. It was an odd feeling. Instead of the pressure she'd experienced in an airplane, which pushed passengers back into the seat, the sudden vertical lift gave the odd sensation of compressing her spine. She forced herself to sit up straighter.

The nose dipped toward the ground and they floated forward. Through the plexiglass bottom of the bubble the pavement slipped away underneath her feet. They rose higher in the air, leaving the cluster of buildings behind, and negotiated a range of small hills studded with microwave and cellular towers.

Alex controlled the craft using both hands and feet, his movements deft and sure. Once firmly on course, he looked over.

"What do you think?" His voice came directly into her ears through the headphones, the motion of his lips strangely disorienting.

She shouted back. "It's fantastic!"

"We should be there in twenty minutes or so." He went back to monitoring the various gauges, and June soon became engrossed with the view out the window. She'd only ever flown in large commercial jets before, and couldn't believe how tremendous the range of sight was without a wing in the way. She spied a moose in an old clear-cut, and watched its long-legged, high-stepping stride with amusement.

They flew into a wide valley, and she spotted a haphazard collection of canvas coloured rectangles. As they closed in, the shapes sorted themselves out into eight to ten large tents, surrounding an even bigger structure with a green striped roof, reminding her of an old-fashioned circus big-top. A figure walked out from underneath it and waited in the grassy area outside the grouping of tents.

Her stomach hovered in her abdomen as the altimeter dropped. Alex, operating the hand levers expertly, lowered the craft into the alpine meadow and shut off the engine. The rotors whined down, and stillness settled over them. A faint buzzing filled her ears.

A tall, thin man wearing a grungy graphic T-shirt, khaki shorts sprouting a multitude of pockets, and a brightly striped toque, waved at them as they stepped out.

"Hello." He extended a hand to Alex. "I'm Ryan Persson. You must be the Wildlife guy."

"And you must be the Camp Manager." Alex introduced himself and June.

Lank, dark blond hair streamed past Ryan's shoulders and his finger nails were chipped and lined with dirt. But his eyes were bright with intelligence under the vibrant cap, and his teeth gleamed whitely in the light stubble on his chin.

"I suppose you'd like to get right out there."

Alex nodded. "Yes. How far do we need to hike?"

Ryan cocked a thumb toward the camp. "I've got a couple of four-wheelers we can use. Beats walking any day."

Soon Alex and June were buckling on borrowed helmets and flipping a coin to see who got to drive the ATV. As June plopped triumphantly into the driver's position, Alex strapped their packs to the carrying grid and mounted behind. Ryan negotiated circumspectly through the camp on his own machine, then picked up speed on a barely visible dirt track.

Despite the serious reason for their journey, June enjoyed the adventure. The ATV wasn't a smooth ride, but it manoeuvred the ruts and rocks with ease. She gave the throttle a burst, and Alex's hold on her waist tightened. A growl of protest rumbled in his chest, pressed against her back. She laughed wickedly and gunned it again.

On the mountainside to her left a logging road zigzagged up the steep incline. This area had been recently harvested for timber, and now the tree planting crew was restocking the forest with native conifers. June had spent a couple of summers as a planter, and had nothing but respect for the men and women who did the work, which required great physical stamina as well as attention to detail.

They came upon one of the planters' temporary bases. A couple of sturdy four by four pickups and a large passenger van were parked at the bottom of a long slope. Dotted about the incline were perhaps twenty men and women. Each carried a shovel with a long, narrow blade, and slung over their shoulders were large canvas bags, rather like the kind old-time paperboys used to carry. The tips of tiny coniferous seedlings poked out of each sack. As the ATVs slowed to go past the vehicles, June had a chance to watch one woman move fluidly through the motions—place shovel, step on blade to sink it into the earth, bend to insert seedling, straighten, press with boot heel to ensure correct planting. The best planters did hundreds of trees in a day.

Once past the workers, they picked up speed, and it wasn't long before Ryan came to a stop near a still, black form. They swung off the ATVs and stood over the desecrated body.

****

Alex sat back on his heels and wiped sweat off his forehead with the back of his wrist.

"Well," he said, "it's like the other."

"Can you tell if it's the same poacher?" June hunkered down beside him. As disturbing as the sight and smell was, it was nowhere near as bad as the other carcass they'd found in the crevasse.

"There are definite similarities, but there's no way to say for sure." Alex gestured at the remains. "Head, paws, gallbladder. I tell you, from their point of view, these guys aren't wasting a thing. They're taking everything they'll get paid for."

"The same poacher?" Ryan Persson had been standing out of the way while Alex inspected the body. Now he moved closer. "You mean you've found other bears?"

Alex told him briefly about the previous discovery. "The thing is, for every body we find, there could be many others out there we know nothing about. I went through our files and found a couple more illegal kills in this area last fall. But just because we've learned of four in the last few months doesn't mean it's the same poacher. This area is full of blacks and grizzlies and will attract more hunters willing to break the rules. Odds are there'd be more to find."

He returned to his work, snapping photos and jotting down notes. June let the mountain stillness wash over her. A raven's call echoed faintly off the far wall of the valley.

He straightened up from the body, snapping off his latex gloves. "This one's a female." Bitterness tinged his voice. "I wonder what..."

"Quiet," June commanded.

Both men looked at her in surprise.

"Listen," she said.

"What is it?"

She shushed Ryan with an abrupt motion of her hand.

"There," she said. "Did you hear that?"

Alex tilted his head. "Over there."

They turned toward a small thicket a few metres away. It was a stand of young birch, no more than ten feet tall, at whose feet a number of shrubs huddled. Something hidden in the shadows caused the brush to rustle and sway. June heard again the fretful sound that had first caught her ear.

"What do we do now?"

Alex turned to Ryan. "I need a length of rope, about three metres long. And a blanket or piece of tarp, something like that."

"I'll check in the four-wheeler." Ryan walked to his

ATV and lifted the lid of the plastic case strapped on the back. He came back with a long piece of yellow nylon rope and a ratty old plaid blanket.

June didn't take her eyes off the subtle movements. Ryan handed the rope to Alex, who wound it in generous loops and hooked it on his elbow. He threw the blanket over his shoulder.

"Okay," he said softly. "I'm going to make a wide circle far around the bush. When I close in behind, I want you both to rush up. We'll roust him out."

They waited, motionless, as Alex strolled casually away. He took up position, unfolded the blanket and held it in front of him, rather like a matador's cape.

Ryan watched June. She nodded, and the quiet of the wilderness shattered with their screams and yells. They ran wildly toward the bushes.

The bear cub's nerve held until they were practically on top of it. Then it shot out the far side, a black ball of fur, squealing and bawling, staring white-eyed over its shoulder. Alex made a diving tackle, and miraculously managed to wrap the cub in the blanket on the first try. Ryan and June ran up and helped him hold the wriggling, squiggling bundle. Piteous whimpers and squeals rent the air.

"Now what?" June asked breathlessly. Despite the cub's small size, it put up a valiant effort to get free, sharp little claws scrabbling at her through the blanket.

"Hold him." Alex pulled the rope off his arm. "I'll get him secured."

After more hectic minutes, they had the cub safely tied up inside the blanket. Alex left its head free, but dropped a noose over its muzzle to stop it biting, causing the cub to growl and hiss in frustration. June had added another scrape to her healing collection, Ryan's toque had come off in the battle, and Alex's neatly pressed uniform was scuffed and bedraggled. They paused for a breather.

"What are you going to do with him?" Ryan panted.

"We'll have to take him with us." Alex sucked the knuckles of his hand where needle-like teeth had gashed him. "We don't really have much choice. He's far too young to survive on his own. There's a wildlife refuge west of Prince George. When we get back to town I'll give Cindy a call and see if she can take him."

"Will he travel all right in the helicopter?" June asked.

"I've got a veterinary kit in the storage compartment," Alex said. "I'll give him a shot of tranquillizer, enough to keep him calm. We should be okay." He looked from the furious little bundle on the ground to the four-wheelers they had arrived on. "But first, we have to get him there."

In the end, June drove the ATV back to camp, with Alex perched precariously behind her, facing backward, cradling the cub on his lap and letting his long legs trail over the rear of the machine. She could feel the muscles in his back flex and strain as he curbed the cub's efforts to get free. Once at the tree planters' camp, Alex dug out a syringe and injected the cub with a minuscule dose. Its whimpers and cries faded away, and even though its eyes remained open, the ferociousness left them, replaced with drowsy bewilderment.

They made a tiny nest in the space behind the pilot's seat, and Alex lifted the bear in. He loosened the noose around its nose, but kept it in place, then turned to Ryan.

"Thanks for your help." They shook hands. "Remember, if anyone sees anything, notices anything that might be relevant, we need to know."

"No problem. Let me know how the little guy makes out."

"I will."

Ryan backed away from the helicopter as Alex and June hoisted themselves into their seats. They rose into the air in a whirl of dust. Her last glimpse of the camp was Ryan shielding his eyes from the flying scatter and the tents flapping in the breeze.

****

The Nechako Home for Rescued Wildlife kept a low profile with the public, but to those in the know like Alex and his colleagues there was no better place to bring a wild animal. He, June and their small companion travelled about half an hour west of Prince George, then turned onto a narrow, gravel road heading north. After fifteen minutes or so, during which time the cub became more and more restless and vocal, it branched off. Keeping to the right, Alex negotiated the Jeep over a rutted, bone-jarring track. Finally the route widened, and he pulled to a stop.

It was an idyllic, albeit rustic, example of the rural beauty of Northern British Columbia. Spreading out before them was a tiny lake, perhaps one kilometre long and half a kilometre wide, bordered by willows and pine trees and edged with marshy, reedy areas. A battered yellow canoe floated next to the dock that T'd into the water from a pebbly beach. To the right a dull red cabin with a wrap-around porch, stone chimney, and metal roof faced the lake. Paint was peeling off the window frames and a number of the slats on the deck railing rested sleepily against each other.

To the left a long, low roofed building, resembling a dog kennel, stretched out into the forest. Instead of the usual domesticated canines, however, the inmates of these runs were their wild cousins, including a number of scruffy foxes and a coyote with three legs. Separate from this structure was an enormous enclosure, two stories high and constructed around a number of living shrubs and two tall spruce, with walls and roof of thick chain link. Alex couldn't see any inhabitants, but he knew it was used to house cougars, lynx and other feral felines. And the occasional bear. Behind these facilities were various corrals, complete with lean-to shelters, water troughs and feeding racks. A doe stood at one of the mangers, calmly chewing hay while her tiny spotted fawn suckled vigorously.

A short, stocky woman carrying a pitchfork loaded with hay came around the corner of the kennel block. They stepped out to meet her.

"For Christ sake, if it ain't Mr. Weaver," she shouted. "Come to ask another goddamn favour, I suppose. Always needs something for nothing." She leaned her pitchfork against the wall and strode forward, continuing at the same volume. "Biggest mooch I've ever seen. Don't know why I bother. Costs me money every time he stops in."

She peered into the tinted windows of the Jeep. "Whatcha got this time? Wolverine? Porcupine? Bald eagle?" She spun toward Alex and poked him in the chest with a gnarled, grimy finger. "It better be good, or you can take it right away with you."

Alex grinned. "Cindy, Cindy, you know you love it when I visit." He wrapped his arm around her wide shoulders and turned her toward June. "I'd like you to meet June Brandt."

"Nice to meet you," Cindy said gruffly, glaring out from pale eyes hiding behind straggling bangs. Alex had seen her in the city one day and had barely recognized her with combed hair, tidy jeans, and clean parka. He was more used to her as she was today. A ratty old fisherman's hat was jammed on her head and tousled, Medusa-like locks of light brown hair snaked out from underneath. The red and black checked flannel jacket and blue coveralls she wore were indescribably dirty, with holes in knees and elbows. On her feet were large rubber gumboots caked in mud and filth.

She elbowed Alex in the ribs. "So, whatcha got? Ain't got all day, you know."

Alex opened the back door of the Jeep and Cindy pushed him aside to see her prize.

"Oh," she crooned, the first sound she'd made not at full volume. "Looky, here, lovey. Mama's got you." She reached in and scooped up the cub, cradling it in her brawny arms.

The cub seemed to recognize a sympathetic presence, and stopped its panicked whining. White still showed around the bark brown of its irises, but the stiff ruff on its neck settled down as it relaxed into Cindy's embrace.

"Shhh," she whispered, rubbing her chin between its ears, "you're gonna be okay now."

Alex smirked at June triumphantly, who stood mouth agape. Without another word, Cindy turned and trudged off to the kennel.

They followed behind, entering the concrete hall in time to see Cindy and her new love disappear through a doorway on the right. They stopped in the entrance. She laid the cub on a straw filled bed on the far side of a chain link fence dividing the space from left to right. With great gentleness and deliberation she unwrapped the blanket and removed the rope from its muzzle, all the while sing-songing in a soothing tone. The cub's gaze never left her face, and even though it was now free to defend itself, it lay quietly, paws curled.

Cindy stepped out of the wire enclosure and closed the gate. She headed across the hall and filled a metal pail with fresh water. Striding back, she unlatched a small opening in the fence and slid the pail into the cub's space, locking it afterward. Only then did her focus return to her human visitors.

"What are you two still doing here?" she blustered, once again at full volume. June flinched, bumping into Alex. "I don't need you anymore, and neither does he. Go on, get."

Alex hugged her. "You're a good woman, Cindy."

"Go on with you," she said brusquely and shoved him away. "If I need you I'll call you." She turned her back on them to beam adoringly at her new charge.

Chapter Six

The vehicle jounced and bounced its way back along the rutted track. Once travelling on the smooth surface of the main highway June turned to Alex. "What the hell was that?"

He laughed. "I thought you'd enjoy meeting Cindy. It's not often you discover someone who knows exactly what she wants. All Cindy wants to do is help animals and stay away from humans. She's very good at both."

The affection in his voice had June laughing back. "How long have you known her?"

"I met her about two years ago, shortly after I moved up here. We'd captured an injured cougar in a rural residential area. It had torn its leg open trying to get through a barb wire fence. We sedated it and had a vet stitch it up, but the doctor didn't have the facilities to keep it, and we didn't want to release it until we made sure there was no infection. She suggested Cindy. She was exactly the same then—had no use for you unless you had four legs or feathers."

They neared the city limits. The sky trumpeted orange and pink and rose and salmon as the sun set behind the hills west of town.

"Are you hungry?" June asked. It had been hours since the granola bar she'd scarfed down during the helicopter ride back from the camp, and she was starving. "If you want, I could probably manage to throw something together at my house. And by I, I mean we."

Alex gave her a sideways smile. "Sounds good. I, I mean, we, could probably handle that."

The street in front of her house was full of vehicles, as it often was in the evening, so June directed Alex to the alley running along the rear of the houses and he pulled into the gravel space behind her home. A greying wooden fence separated the parking area from the lawn of the backyard. They went through the creaking gate and up the narrow path, slippery with the decaying remains of apple blossoms. She unlocked the back door and led him into the kitchen.

She went to throw her pack in her bedroom, and noticed on her way through the living room the red light flashing on her land line. She set a large pot of water on the stove and rummaged through the fridge. "How does pasta and salad grab you?"

"Right by my taste buds," Alex answered. "What can I do?"

"Why don't you pour us some wine? Glasses are in the cupboard next to the sink." She put a head of romaine on the counter. "Then you can rip this up and give it a wash. I do a mean Caesar dressing from scratch, but it needs to sit overnight, so this time you'll have to live with store bought." She set a bottle on the counter. "And while you're doing that, if you don't mind, I'm going to check my messages."

She punched in the code, and Richard Fleetham's baritone voice asked her to call him on his cell. She erased the message and dialled.

He answered on the first ring.

"Richard," she said, "June returning your call."

Alex came from the kitchen and handed her a glass.

He stood hip-shot against the door jamb and sipped his wine. His uniform was rumpled and creased from the tussle with the bear cub and his dark hair fell messily over his forehead. He looked so good she lost her train of thought and didn't hear Richard's reply. She scrambled to catch up. "I, uh, got your message."

"Yes, I called for a couple of reasons. One was to see how you were doing after all the excitement recently. Seen any more of your conservation officer?"

Her gaze travelled up and down Alex's length and his eyes narrowed at her scrutiny. "Yes, I have seen more of him. In fact, we spent the day together at another kill site." She told Richard of the day's developments.

After a pause Richard said sorrowfully, "June, June. I asked you to stay safe."

She swallowed irritation. "Helping Alex isn't dangerous, Richard. And besides, I really enjoy it. I'm thinking of asking him for a full-time job." Alex saluted her with his wineglass, and she winked back.

She waited through another short silence. "I can't keep you from doing what you want," Richard said, "but I have another project you might like to take on. Not quite as exciting, of course." He gave a throaty chuckle. "RiverForce has received a small government grant to hire a part-time administration assistant over the summer, to get our files in order and do some organizing, nothing strenuous. I thought of you right away."

"Me?"

"Why not you? You're bright, interested and a university student who, I assume, needs the experience and the money. If you don't want it, however..."

"No, that's not what I meant. Of course I'll take it. When do you want me to start?"

"I know it's short notice, but how's tomorrow? I'll be at the university and can set you up with everything you need. Meet me at my office...say ten a.m.?"

"That will work." Aware she didn't sound particularly excited, she injected her voice with more enthusiasm. "Thanks again, Richard, for thinking of me. I appreciate it."

"No problem, no problem at all," he replied, and broke the connection.

She gave Alex a quick rundown while she thawed shrimp under cool water. "I suppose I should be more grateful," she said with a shrug, "but it seems very odd he would offer it to me. There's a fellow called Thomas in the group that would do it all for free...probably is doing it already for free. Getting paid would make him think he's died and gone to heaven." She pulled out a cutting board and knife. "But I'm not one to turn down easy money. Thomas will have to suffer."

She minced onion and garlic, then sautéed it with olive oil and added the shrimp. While it simmered she added fettuccine to the water. Alex finished the salad, and she told him where to find plates and silverware and he set the kitchen table. When the pasta was tender and the shrimp deliciously pink, she tossed it all with a hefty sprinkle of freshly grated Parmesan cheese and served it up in a brightly coloured pottery dish.

They slurped the fettuccine noisily and peeled the shrimp with their fingers. She was tinglingly aware of her knees grazing his under the table.

June put away leftovers as Alex ran hot water, then

they stood side by side and did the dishes together, shoulders bumping occasionally. After she dried the last pot, Alex took the towel from her hands. She leaned against the counter. His deep brown eyes, keen and glowing, met hers, and an answering heat lit deep within her. He draped the towel over her head, around her neck and pulled her forward until their bodies were almost touching. June's pulse beat heavily and her eyes dropped to his mouth. He rested his forehead against hers. His breath feathered her cheek, scented with the wine they'd shared.

She closed her eyes. "What do you want to do now?"

He laughed deep in his chest. "I don't know. What do you want to do?"

"We could watch TV."

He kissed the tip of her nose. "We could."

"Or go for a walk."

His lips shifted to the corner of her mouth. "Sounds good."

"Then again," she murmured, and let her head fall back, "we could do something else."

"I vote for that," he said, and lowered his mouth to hers.

Blood raced through her veins, blooming in her belly, searing through her centre. His lips were warm, demanding, and he coaxed her mouth open with his tongue. She tasted a hint of spice, and his own unique maleness.

Releasing the ends of the towel, his hands drifted down, skimming the sides of her breasts. He pulled her forward, holding her hips firmly against his, his hardness pressing into her. She wound her arms around his neck, and her fingers threaded through his hair as she dove deeper into the kiss.

His hand found her small, firm breast. Pinwheels whirled behind her eyes. His palm burned through the thin material of her T-shirt and bra, and her nipple stiffened. A whimper escaped her lips. When his thumb rubbed across the taut nub, she wrapped her arms even tighter around his neck, desperate for balance.

In one movement, he hoisted her onto the counter, then swept his hands under her shirt over the flushed skin of her ribs. Lifting the material, he slipped down the white cotton of her bra and dipped his head.

She was afraid she might melt away, so intense was the pull of his mouth. She felt it on her breast, and tugging throughout her body, deep into her core. Her hands grasped his head, holding him close.

His fingers grappled with the button on her jeans. She stiffened as the backs of his fingers brushed low on her stomach.

"No," she panted. "Wait."

Her hands gripped his. He raised his head and stared at her with hooded eyes.

She slid off the counter, pulling her T-shirt down. His arms encircled her, drawing her tight to his body. "Don't let go," she said, voice hoarse with desire. "I don't think I can stand on my own yet."

She tucked her head under his chin, breathing in the subtle scent of his aftershave. His heart beat an uneven tattoo under her cheek, and she was glad he was as deeply affected as she. He loosened her hair from its untidy knot, and spread the strands over her shoulders, running his fingers through it, soothing them both.

"I think we know where this could go," she said, her

breath whispering against his neck.

"Straight to the bedroom," he said decisively.

She giggled softly, then sighed. "But not tonight."

The hand weaving through her hair stilled. He drew back and tugged gently, lifting her head to meet his gaze, where the desire and demand still burned.

"Why not?"

She sucked in a deep breath, and stepped away from him, standing on her own. "I am attracted to you." She blew a gust of air out, fluttering the hair hanging about her face. "And how stupid does that sound, considering. But I'm not going to sleep with you tonight."

His eyes narrowed. "You want to. You can't deny that."

"I do want to. More than you know. But I can't."

"Of course you can. What I want to know is why you won't."

She was surprised by the depth of annoyance in his voice. "Because I'm not looking for a short term fling...I'm looking for more. We only met a couple of weeks ago. We've only seen each other a few times. I'm not ready."

He closed off immediately, tense, cold, all emotions clamped tight. "What do you mean, more?"

"More time. More chances to get to know you." She twisted her fingers together. "More commitment."

"Commitment?" he choked. "You said it yourself, we barely know each other, and you want commitment?" She held tight to her composure, afraid she might crumple beneath the fiery anger in his words, the flare of antagonism in his eyes. "I want to take you, find out how you like to be touched, the noises you'll make when I please you. But that's all I'm offering.

Pleasure, not promises."

Turning away, she opened a cupboard, took out a glass, and filled it with water from the tap. "I see." She took a small sip, and another, trying to soothe the burning at the back of her throat where tears threatened.

"For God's sake, what do you want from me?" He paced the small kitchen. "I could have had you right here, but you asked me to stop. I did. And now you're telling me...what? What exactly are you telling me, June?"

"I'm sorry." She clutched the counter behind her back so tightly the edge cut into her fingers. "I'm not trying to be a tease. I'm trying to be honest."

"Maybe I should leave." He glared across the room. "Maybe I should go."

"I don't want you to leave. But I'm not going to have sex with you tonight."

Silence stretched between them.

Slowly the fierceness in his expression faded. He breathed deeply through his nose, once, twice. "You have no idea what you do to me, do you?" He approached her cautiously. "But if you're being honest with me, the least I can do is be honest with you."

Keeping a safe space between them, he mirrored her position at the counter. "Your parents are still together, right?" She nodded, watching his profile. "Mine split when I was thirteen. My dad divorced wife number three last year, and is now with a woman younger than I am. My mother hasn't re-married, but she continues to have a succession of men-friends." His voice was sour, his face grim. "It took me a long time to realize they were having their flings on the side long before they divorced. Commitment? Not something I'm used to."

She wanted to reach out, comfort him in some way, erase the desolation of the boy inside the man. "You don't believe a man and a woman can love each other, forever?"

He lifted his shoulders in an irritable shrug. "Happily ever after? Really? What kind of fairy tale are you living in?"

She refused to be hurt. Instead, she said lightly, "See, this is exactly my point."

"What?"

"These are the things I want to know about you, need to know about you. Before we take this any further."

"You certainly seem to know what you want." He took his jacket down from the hook by the back door. "Now I have to decide what I want."

The snick of the latch as he closed the door behind him was the loneliest sound she'd ever heard.

Chapter Seven

"And this," Thomas said sulkily as he pulled open another meticulously organized cabinet drawer, "is where you'll find all the agendas and minutes of our meetings."

She'd never seen file folders so precisely aligned, with colour coded labels and finicky printing that would have made a kindergarten teacher envious. That was, she'd never seen file folders like that except in all the other painstakingly ordered drawers Thomas had shown her during the last half hour.

The original plan had been for June to meet Richard at his office, but when she'd arrived, promptly at ten o'clock, his secretary had sent her on to the RiverForce office, saying Thomas was waiting for her and Richard would join them as soon as he finished a meeting that "he just couldn't put off."

The thirty minutes she'd spent with Tubby Tom, as Tabitha maliciously dubbed him, was twenty-five minutes too long. He appeared to covet the job Richard had given her beyond all reason, and it was getting on her nerves. To do him justice, she couldn't help but wonder what Richard was thinking as well. She'd never seen a better organized office, and she had no idea how he expected her to fill even the measly ten hours a week she was scheduled to work.

"I don't understand," Thomas muttered morosely

for what seemed like the twentieth time. "I don't understand why Richard needed to hire someone to do this."

"Neither do I," June said, exasperated enough to be brutally truthful. "But thanks for showing me around." She sat behind the desk. "I'm sure you've got all sorts of other things you'd rather be doing. I think I'm all set." She smiled encouragingly and repeated, "Thanks," resisting the urge to make shooing motions.

"I thought I'd stick around until Richard got here," Thomas replied. "See if he needs anything."

She was beginning to doubt the man's sanity. Why was he so desperate to stick around when he had to know he wasn't needed? A small wedge of sympathy edged past the aggravation. "I'm going to get typing the agenda for the next meeting. Stay if you want to." She wiggled the computer mouse and opened the blank agenda file. Working off an email Richard had sent previously, she began filling in the details, resolutely ignoring the heavy sighs coming from Thomas.

They were still in their own little bubbles when Richard burst in a few minutes later.

"Ah, I'm glad to see you both still here. Thomas, thanks so much for showing June the ropes." He patted the younger man on the shoulder, but the gesture was shrugged off.

"Richard," Thomas said stiffly, "I'd like to speak with you for a moment."

"Of course, of course," Richard said in his hearty manner. "What can I do for you?"

"Not here," Thomas said. "I'd like to speak with you in private."

"Certainly. Let's go to my office, shall we? It'll

give us a chance to discuss the major project I want you to take on."

Thomas' gloom evaporated. "You've got a project for me?" His eyes lit up and his entire manner changed from pouting to pompous.

"Of course I do," Richard boomed. "Why else did I hire June? So you would have time for your new duties." He clapped Thomas on the back, and this time the younger man blushed at the attention. "June, we'll go over more details after I've talked with Thomas. Any questions right now?"

She wasn't about to ask how the heck she was going to keep occupied with Thomas right there, so she shook her head and turned to the computer. In no time at all, she was done with the agenda. She emailed a copy to Richard for his approval, then called up the minutes from the last meeting, which Thomas had already typed, emailed them to everyone in the group, and printed one copy, which she posted on the bulletin board.

And was done.

She surveyed the tiny room. From where she stood, with her back against the wall immediately opposite the door, the desk was to her right, facing into the room, with a window behind it overlooking a shipping and loading dock. On the left was a row of three filing cabinets, Thomas's pride and joy. Various posters tried limply to enliven the institutional beige paint.

Idly she opened a filing drawer, vaguely hoping to find something to do. Inside were folders with labels such as "Itinerary — Fleetham, Richard", "Trade Fairs" and "School Visits". She pulled out the itinerary folder and found various sheets tucked together tidily with silver paper clips. The one on top was dated the beginning of May, before June had met Alex on top of Longworth Mountain, and gave a list of transportation details, hotel accommodations, and conference seminars in regards to a trip Richard had made to Vancouver.

She slipped the folder back in its slot, slid the drawer shut and was thinking about checking Facebook to kill time when her cell phone buzzed.

****

Alex would have suffered untold tortures before admitting to anyone how many times he'd changed his mind about calling June.

He had been upset and aroused, disappointed and disturbed when he'd left her house last night. Kissing her, touching her, had set off a firestorm inside him. He still had her scent in his nostrils—soap and fresh air and something even more basic, more primal, he couldn't define. When she'd asked him to stop, to wait, he'd struggled for the control she'd wanted from him, but had been willing to slow things down. The need for her had pumped through his system as he'd waited impatiently for her to invite him to her bed.

And then she'd told him no.

It wasn't that he couldn't handle rejection. But he'd never wanted to be with a woman as strongly as he wanted to be with June. When she told him she wasn't ready, wanted more time to decide, something very much like panic had balled in his gut, and desire had faded into fear. He'd hid behind anger, until her stricken face extinguished his fury.

It had taken a severe act of will to head out into the night. Tall and slim, she had beckoned to him like a flame in the dark, but he couldn't let himself go to her. Wouldn't, until he knew what he wanted from her. Was able to give her what she wanted from him.

One sleepless night had made him realize he hadn't walked away from her for good. If she needed time, he'd give it to her.

As long as she gave him another chance.

The phone rang so many times he worried it was going to voice mail. When she finally answered, he spoke briskly, striving to hide his nervousness. "How's the new gig?"

At first he thought she wasn't going to answer. When she did, her tone was blandly polite. "It's fine, thank you."

"Good, that's good." More silence at the other end of the line. Alex drew in a deep breath and felt fifteen again. The worst of it was he deserved the treatment he was getting. "I'm sorry," he said bluntly. "I want to apologize. I acted like a jerk last night."

"We both needed to say some things, and we did. Now we know where we stand."

Alex gazed unseeingly out his office window. She didn't sound welcoming, but at least she was talking to him. "I don't usually react that way when a woman tells me 'no.'"

"I don't imagine it has happened too many times."

A hint of warmth coloured her voice. A powerful wave of relief swept through him. "Maybe it should happen more often." He hurried on. "I want to see you again. Soon."

"I'd like that. I'd like that very much."

"I've got a meeting tonight I can't miss. Iain Provost...remember him, you met him that day at the office..." she made a noise of assent "...has arranged a big get together about the McGregor kills to brainstorm a direction for us. And I'm scheduled to be on call the next two days, so I'm not supposed to leave town. But Iain owes me a couple of favours. Let me see if I can get him to cover for me. If I can swing that, could you arrange to come hiking with me? I'm thinking of heading to Fort George Canyon."

"I should probably ask Richard about my schedule first, but I can't see why he would mind. I'll let you know."

"June?"

"Yes?"

"Thanks for taking my call."

****

June dropped her phone back in her bag. The hard knot that had taken up residence in her stomach after last evening dissolved as she'd listened to Alex's apology. She'd been so afraid she'd put an end to their relationship practically before it began.

Richard re-entered the office.

"All set?" White teeth flashed in the dark, neat beard.

"I guess so." She hesitated, then plunged in. "I've got to ask, Richard. What exactly do you want me to do while I'm here? Thomas seems to have everything wrapped up."

"I've given Thomas a project that will keep him very busy over the next few weeks. He's going to be redesigning the RiverForce website. I managed to get a grant for that, as well, so he'll be paid for his work."

That was great news. She'd wondered whether Thomas would be breathing down her neck every day.

Richard continued. "You'll keep up with the correspondence, update the newsletter, send out emails, you know, the regular things Thomas was doing."

"All right then. Do you expect me to be in the office every day?"

"No, no, of course not. I trust you to adjust your schedule as needed. Some days will be busier than others, I'm sure."

"I would imagine so." Although busy might be stretching it. "Should I let you know if I'm not coming in one day?"

Richard chuckled. "Planning time off with your friend, the CO, already?"

His obvious amusement nettled her, and she answered brusquely. "Not necessarily. He's actually scheduled to work the next couple of days." It was none of Richard's business, after all.

"If you are going to miss a day or so, an email would be great. My schedule is posted on the university server, or you can always check with my office, if you need to get a hold of me. Now, about the next meeting..." He went on to cover a few points of business regarding the agenda she'd sent him. "Obviously, there's no hurry, so if you make those changes before the end of the week that will be fine." He nodded at the wall clock. "And I see you've been here a couple of hours, so your first day is done."

"I guess so." She smiled at him. "Thanks, Richard. I really do appreciate the opportunity."

"No problem at all." Once again she felt the force of his charm as he smiled back at her. "I always like to keep my eye on my RiverForce members."

****

June's plans were virtuous as she left the campus. A free afternoon and evening would give her the chance to catch up on chores around the house. But the weather was brilliantly sunny, with a hint of a refreshing breeze. It was much too nice a day to waste on laundry and sweeping floors.

Minutes after parking her pickup behind her house, she headed out the front door, dressed in running gear.

Turning right on the sidewalk, she walked past neatly trimmed lawns and charmingly tended houses, and into one of the city's largest green spaces. Set above the muddy brown rush of the Fraser River, Fort George Park was the original location of the Hudson Bay Company's fur trading post.

She broke into a jog, cutting straight across a wide open grassy expanse, heading for the trail along the riverbank. The muscles in her legs stretched and flexed, and she embraced the sensation of a well-tuned body. Soon the rhythm took over, and her consciousness was free to float.

Inevitably, Alex filled her mind. Hearing him talk about his childhood had helped her understand his attitude, but it was her own reaction that worried her most.

She had never had to deal with feelings and desires like those Alex stirred up inside her. If she had to decide between sleeping with him to keep him, or losing him altogether, she was no longer sure what she might choose.

She flowed smoothly along, breathing regular and even, muscles loose and limber. She stayed with the trail as it crossed under the big four lane bridge that carried the highway east and the old railway drawbridge.

Now it curved left and travelled beside the Nechako River, a smaller tributary which entered the Fraser from the west. Her feet padded on the wood chip path as it twisted through tall cottonwoods.

She reached the halfway mark of her run, a little rocky open space right down on the river's edge underneath yet another bridge. There she took a breather, making sure to drink water and check her time. Then she turned around and headed back.

The first thing she noticed when she walked in the house was the blinking light on her phone. She punched in the code.

Her mother's voice filled the room. "We're back, June. Got in about half an hour ago. Had a good time visiting Jake. We'd love to see you. Give us a call."

She dialed her parent's number and her dad answered. "How was the drive?" she asked.

"Good, good. No trouble at all. I'll get your mother."

She grinned. Not one for small talk, her dad.

She made noncommittal noises as her mother chattered about their week in Vancouver, which they'd spent visiting their son, who was taking his law degree at the University of British Columbia, and a number of old friends.

She juggled the phone between chin and shoulder as she pulled off her sweaty running clothes and tossed them in the hamper. Walking in her underwear from bedroom to bathroom, she managed to catch a break in the conversation.

"Mom, why don't I drive out tonight and you can tell me all about it?" She pulled the phone away from her ear to check the time on its display. "Or, better yet, why don't I come for dinner? I just got in from a run, so I have to shower, and I desperately need to throw in a load of laundry, but I can come by in a couple of hours. Do you need me to bring anything?"

"We stopped at the grocery store on our way through town, so we should be good. See you in a bit then."

Chapter Eight

Alex was leaving Iain's office, where they had been preparing for the meeting later that day, when his cell rang. He did his best to suppress the hope it was June. He'd spoken to her a few hours ago, for Pete's sake. Surely he was able to survive longer than that before needing to talk to her again?

His heart sank when he read the display. He closed his office door and blew out a deep breath before making the connection.

"Hello, Dad." He dropped into his chair.

"I've got great news, son." Dylan Weaver had the educated, buttery tones of a national radio announcer, the confidence of a self-made man, and the morals of an alley cat. He'd been married three times, and, Alex believed, had been monogamous for extremely short periods during each. He seemed to find it impossible to say no to any woman who fluttered her eyelashes at him. And even though he was well into his fifties, his refined good looks and well-stocked financial portfolio continued to attract females. "Sondra and I are getting married."

Alex rubbed his thumb deep into his eye socket. He'd met his father's current girlfriend, now fiancée, once, but he wouldn't soon forget her overtly enhanced hair, teeth and breasts. The three of them had had dinner together last summer when Alex was in Vancouver for a few days. It was seared in his memory as one of the most awkward meals of his life.

"Congratulations," he said colourlessly.

Ignoring Alex's lacklustre response, Dylan went on. "Sondra wants me to invite you to our engagement party." Not "we" want to invite you, Alex noted. "She insisted, in fact. It's going to be in a couple of weeks." His father's tone was not welcoming. Alex was the last person his father wanted near Sondra. He might have suspect taste in women, but he wasn't stupid.

Dinner had started innocently enough. Alex had plenty of practice meeting the various women who had passed through his father's life. When he'd been younger, he'd thought of them as possible step-mothers, but after he'd experienced the drama and trials of his father's second divorce he'd lowered his expectations. Now all he wished for was someone he could stand being in the same room with.

At first he'd thought the contact was accidental. Sondra and his father sat across the table from him, and she appeared to be concentrating entirely on whatever pompous theory his father was spouting. Then her bare toes slipped under the cuff of his trouser leg and brushed sexily up and down his shin. Her dark-rimmed eyes met his boldly, and she slicked the tip of her tongue wetly between her lips.

He'd tucked his legs uncomfortably under his chair, out of her reach. Yet that hadn't stopped her from making subtle, sensuous motions every time she had his attention. He wasn't sure when Dylan noticed his girlfriend was flirting with his son, but by the end of the evening a pulse beat thickly in his temple, and he'd rushed Sondra out of the restaurant.

"I don't know about that, Dad. Things are kind of busy at work."

"I told Sondra you probably wouldn't have time." Alex heard the relief. A familiar but faded sense of failure twisted through him. Like many children of divorced parents, he'd thought if he'd been a better son, worked harder at school, done something, anything differently, he could have kept his family together. He'd stopped blaming himself years ago, but that didn't mean he didn't wish, once in a while, life had turned out otherwise.

"I'm sorry I can't make it. I'll come to the wedding."

"You'll have plenty of time to arrange that. This is Sondra's first marriage. She wants to make it spectacular."

"I'm sure it will be." He should have offered his father best wishes. He couldn't. "Good luck," he said. Only after he rang off did he add a truly sincere comment. "You'll need it."

****

June hopped into her truck for the short drive to her parent's home, on a five acre parcel of property a few kilometres east of the city. They had bought the land a couple of years ago, and had built themselves a log house. But not just any log house.

Her little old pickup laboured up the steep hill leading out of the river valley that held the city centre. Traffic was heavy, and while a silver SUV seemed content enough to follow, other vehicles passed her easily as she kept to the outside lane.

When the highway leveled out, June picked up speed. A couple of minutes later, she took the left hand turn leading to her parent's rural subdivision. The vehicle behind also made the turn. The road narrowed, twisting between tall stands of pale-green-skinned poplar and slender birch. At random intervals driveways cut through the forest, but most of the houses to which they led were hidden.

She checked her mirror again. The SUV was still behind her, now aggressively hugging her bumper. "Why didn't you pass me on the hill if you're in such a hurry," she muttered. Her parent's driveway came into view, so she flicked on her indicator and tapped her brakes, hoping the other driver would get the message and back off before she turned left. Instead, she heard the roar of acceleration and the SUV dodged into the oncoming lane, racing past her. Heavily tinted windows prevented her from seeing inside, but didn't stop her from making a furious gesture she hoped the driver would see. "Jerk!" she yelled, adrenalin rushing. "Thanks for nothing!"

She carefully negotiated the narrow driveway. One final turn brought her parent's home in sight, and the last traces of temper drained away. She wanted to laugh every time she saw the log house, and today was no exception.

Using large trees cleared from the property, her father had cut logs into three foot lengths, then laid them in a circle pattern with the butt ends facing out. Sealing them together, he had raised multiple layers. Then, with the truly enormous trunk of a cedar as the centre pole, he had completed the round structure with a shake roof.

June pulled to a stop, struck as always by the unusual polka dotted exterior. Her parents had been forced to settle for boring rectangular doorways, but the windows were portholes and gave the whole odd structure a nautical feel. Planted in the middle of a grassy lawn, flower beds were beginning to green up all around its circular walls. It seemed to have sprung, fully formed, from the ground.

Hiding behind a thick hedge made from ruthlessly pruned spruce trees was a much more mundane double garage, with one large roll-up door open and a light shining inside. As she walked toward it, her father slammed shut the tailgate and closed the lid of the canopy on his truck.

"Good timing." He held out an armful of shopping bags. "You can help carry your mother's stuff in." No visit to Vancouver was complete unless her mother had at least one good spending spree.

"Hi, Dad." She gave him a quick peck. "Looks like she did well this trip."

"You know your mother."

Although born in Canada, his voice often held the light echo of his parents' German origin. Karl Brandt had made his living working in one of the pulp and paper mills that were Prince George's main revenue base. Not quite six feet tall, his lean build hadn't softened when he took early retirement. He favoured flannel shirts in muted plaids and well-worn jeans, and had enjoyed taking his children on camping trips to remote lakes when they were growing up. She wondered if he was disappointed two of his oldest sons had left for bigger cities, and seemed to be embracing lifestyles so different from the way they had been raised.

She bumped her shoulder into his as they walked companionably across the yard. "How's Jacob?"

He shrugged. "He's got a job for the summer

clerking in a law office. Not much money, but he seems to like it."

"It won't be long before he can get an articling position. Then he'll make more."

"It's not me that's worried. It's your mother."

She juggled the handles of the bags so she could open the door and let her father through before her. According to Karl, he never worried about anything, but his wife worried about a lot.

"I know you've been helping him out, like you help me by not charging proper rent for the house. I guess you're lucky Sean and Matthew didn't want to keep going to school. It's too soon to tell with Zachary." She added in a teasing tone, "We might have put you in the poor house."

Karl gave her a quiet look. "You know we're happy to help in any way we can."

She placed the parcels on the floor with relief. "Oh, Dad." She gave him a hug. "I know you are. And don't worry," she said lightly, "we'll do our best to keep you in the style to which you've become accustomed. You know, when you're old and decrepit."

Karl smiled at her nonsense.

Dominating every part of the house was the giant cedar trunk supporting the dome-like roof. To the left, a hallway curved around, with rooms along the outside, each with at least one porthole window. To the right, the space was open, with a sitting area leading into a dining area leading into the kitchen. The outer walls, dotted by the butt ends of logs, were mellowed by the tapestries June's mother favoured over framed artwork. Squishy leather furniture surrounded a low table made from a giant burl, and tall leafy plants formed an unusual divider between the living room and eating/kitchen space.

A large mound of brown fur sprawled on a battered and beaten floor cushion. Its dust mop of a tail beat a soft tattoo.

"Is that all the welcome I get, Bauer?" She bent over and ruffled the long hair hanging over the sad brown eyes. "You won't even get up to say hello?"

"He's getting old." Her father sank into his accustomed place on the couch and reached for a beer waiting for him.

June headed to the kitchen, where her mother was standing next to the stove, stirring a large pot. Almost as tall as her husband, Monica was as fair as he was dark, sharing her colouring with her only daughter, while their sons had taken after their father.

"Hello, there." June sniffed the deliciousness rising from the pot. "You're barely been home. How'd you have time to make soup?"

"I know you have a freezer." Monica handed June the spoon to take over. "I've seen it. Full of TV dinners."

"Are you saying I can't cook?"

"Oh, I know you can cook," Monica said sweetly, patting June's cheek as she passed by on her way to set the table. "I also know you don't do it very often."

The three of them sat down to a dinner of homemade turkey soup and fresh multigrain bread from a local bakery.

As Monica handed over a steaming bowl, she took a closer look at June. "Is that a scrape on your chin?"

June reached up to touch the mark on her face. While her bruises were practically healed, the road rash was still faintly visible, although it no longer bothered her and she tended to forget about it.

By the time she'd filled her parents in on everything, beginning with Alex's arrival at Longworth, glossing over getting knocked down by a rogue motorcyclist, and ending with the capture of the bear cub yesterday, they'd finished the meal and were sitting with coffee in the living room.

"Oh, yeah, one more thing," she said, "I also have a part time job with RiverForce this summer."

"Doing what?" asked Karl.

"Working in the office. It's going to be boring, I think."

"Will it keep you away from poachers?"

"Oh, Dad." June shook her head. "You're as bad as Richard. I got the feeling yesterday he offered me the job partly to keep me away from Alex."

"I'm still not sure why he took you along on the second trip."

"He knew I was interested. After all, it is connected to my studies. There's nothing else to it."

Monica raised an eyebrow. "Really?"

To June's surprise a blush heated her cheeks. "How do you do that! Okay, okay. Alex and I have been seeing each other. We've had one date and last night we had dinner at my place." Her good spirits faded slightly when she recalled how the evening ended, although she regarded their upcoming hike with cautious optimism.

Monica was curled up next to Karl, his arm around her shoulders, and June regarded them fondly. "You two have spoiled me, because whenever I'm with someone I compare them to what you have," she said with a touch of longing.

"Are we going to have a chance to meet him?"

"I don't know yet. We're still getting to know each other."

"We're having a barbeque on Friday. Sean and Hillary will be here with Brian, and Zach, of course. A couple more won't make that much difference."

"We'll see, Mom, we'll see." She tucked her feet up, wiggling into a comfy position on the soft-cushioned couch. "Now, tell me more about your trip."

****

No streetlights illuminated the winding road, and the dark was deep and velvet. Her headlights cut a dim swath, barely brightening the ditches. June kept a wary watch for the glimmering green that might be the eyes of a bear, moose or deer, ready to brake if one of them wandered into her path.

While she loved her truck, it wasn't the most comfortable of rides. Tonight it seemed especially rough, with a new vibration shivering through the frame. Maybe it was time to bring her baby in for some work.

As she followed a bend in the road, the shuddering increased dramatically. The steering wheel twisted violently. Making a grab for it, she clamped on and resisted the impulse to stomp on the brakes. An ear-rending screech pulsed through her bones.

The truck headed for the ditch. She fought to keep it on the road.

After anxious ages the truck's momentum slowed. Hesitantly she tapped the brakes, easing onto the shoulder. She shoved it into park with a shaking hand. Her heart throbbed in her throat, making it difficult to breathe. She sat, waiting for calm, until she felt steady enough to step out and assess the situation.

The right front tire was a limp, shapeless piece of rubber, and the truck tilted drunkenly as it rested on the rim.

She'd never experienced a flat tire before and blamed herself for not noticing the symptoms. She kicked the dirt, then cursed when she connected with a buried rock. Limping to the back, she let down the tailgate, climbed in, and rummaged in the toolbox behind the cab for the jack.

She could have called her father. But she'd gotten herself into the mess, and she was going to get herself out.

It was maddening, frustrating work. The jack kept slipping in the scrabbly gravel, but she finally got it secure enough to support the front end. She had to hold her flashlight in her teeth to see what she was doing. The nuts were so tight she needed all her body weight to loosen them, and then she lost one in the long grass of the ditch and had to grovel around for it.

By now she was so aggravated she wouldn't have accepted help if the Michelin Man himself had offered it. Not that anyone was around. She hadn't seen another vehicle since she'd left her parents.

The rusted hub refused to budge. She vented her frustration by bashing the spare tire against it, trying to loosen it. Nothing. Throwing the spare down in disgust, she rested one arm on the passenger side mirror and leaned her forehead on it. After a couple of deep breaths, she bent over for another assault on the hub.

The crash of a gunshot fractured the night. She spun on her heel and stared wild-eyed into the blackness of the forest. The explosion echoed. Terror prickled on her skin.

Was she overreacting? She was in a rural area, after all. Gunshots were a common sound.

Then she saw the small round hole in the fender. It hadn't been there a second ago.

She flung herself into the ditch.

The pickup's windows thundered into fragments.

Chapter Nine

The brainstorming meeting had gone on longer than expected. Alex had barely kicked off his shoes and flopped onto the couch, ready to spend what remained of the evening in front of the TV, when his phone rang. He almost ignored it, until he saw it was June.

"I need you. Please come." Her voice was breathless, shaky.

He snapped to a sitting position. "What's wrong?"

"Someone shot at me. I need you."

He flew out the door of his condo. "Are you hurt? Are you shot?"

"No."

"Where are you?" She gave him directions between hiccoughing sobs. Diving into his Jeep, he took the phone away from his ear only long enough to set up the hands free system. "Have you called 911?"

"Yes. The police are here. I had to stay on the line. They wouldn't let me call you."

"It's okay. I'll be there. I'm on my way."

He blew through a red light at a deserted intersection. His knuckles were white on the wheel, but his voice was calm. He kept June talking as he barreled through town, weaving through the sparse traffic. Once he hit the highway he punched the accelerator. She told him where to turn onto the secondary road. Minutes later he screeched to a stop near a medley of emergency vehicles.

"I'm here. Where are you?"

"The ambulance."

He jumped out, striding toward the red and white vehicle. The back doors were open, and June sat, washed in strobing lights, clutching a tan blanket over her shoulders. A paramedic crouched before her with his hand on her knee. She saw Alex approaching and for a moment her face crumpled, then, throwing off the blanket, she raced into his arms. The feel of her, warm and whole, had relief rolling over him.

He cradled her face in his hands. "Are you sure you're okay?"

"Just petrified."

"What the hell happened?"

They sat on the bumper of the ambulance as June told her story. A pair of police officers searched the cab of her pickup, while the flickering flashes of brilliant LED's indicated others deep in the woods.

"Do you want to go back to your parents?"

She nodded. Adrenalin had kept her on her feet until now, but she was clearly fading. Her head drooped on her slender neck, muscles slack under the palm he had curled around her nape.

Alex stopped one of the RCMP members to tell him where he was taking June. Then he helped her to the Jeep and followed the simple instructions to her parent's home.

She introduced him, but Karl and Monica were so intent on their daughter they barely glanced at him. He stayed long enough to see her settled, then excused himself. As he closed the door, his last sight was of June, eyes shut, head on her father's shoulder, her mother rubbing her back.

****

The sun was shining with unseasonable heat as Alex and June stepped out of his Jeep in the otherwise empty parking lot at the head of the trail to Fort George Canyon.

Their hiking trip had been delayed by a day, but June refused to let him cancel it all together. She was also refusing to make other concessions. Her parents had wanted her to stay with them, yet she had returned to her own home the next morning. She'd even gone into the RiverForce office for a couple of hours. He didn't know whether to be pissed or proud at her stubbornness.

During the drive out, she updated him on the investigation. The police believed the shooter had fired from a small, disused gravel pit overlooking the stretch of road where she had pulled to a stop. A person belly-down on the bank would have had a good view. An examination of the tire revealed a tear, but the tread was so old and worn it was possible it had simply ripped open under stress. Coupled with the motorcycle assault, however, the investigators were decidedly skeptical when June insisted she had no idea who might be making her a target.

"Anyway, enough of that." She pulled her small day pack from the rear seat, and he slung his own over his shoulder. "We're here to enjoy ourselves." She threaded her long ponytail through the back of a bright yellow ball cap. A large bumblebee decorated the crown.

Alex eyed it warily. "Nice hat."

"My nephew gave it to me," she said, slightly defensive. "His name is Brian, and I call him Bee. He's three."

“Ah. That explains it.” He snapped the brim down over those sparkling eyes, and set off on the five kilometre hike to the canyon.

Alex let June set the pace, following behind her on the well-trod path. A comfortable silence descended. The sun dappled through the fresh new poplar and birch leaves, and squirrels chittered constantly. They crossed tiny rivulets and ducked under shadowy spruce. Alex inhaled the scent of rising sap and the dampness of spring thaw lingering in the shadows.

He swung over a winter deadfall blocking the path. June was waiting for him, and he took her hand. They strolled along, linked together, until the trail narrowed and they had to go single file again.

It took about an hour to reach the plateau above the canyon. This section of the Fraser River was a traditional place for First Nations people to fish for salmon. European explorers soon learned the canyon was a treacherous place, with rushing currents, foaming whirlpools and rocky dangers lurking below the surface of the silty brown water. In the early 1900’s, when stern wheelers were still in regular use, passengers would have to disembark and portage around, while the boat itself was winched through the narrow rapids.

They paused at the top of the long drop down. A stout wooden staircase clung to the side of the cliff wall, leading to the worn pinnacles of volcanic rock jutting out of the river. The flow was relatively high, with spring runoff swelling its volume.

“It’s quite the sight, isn’t it.” Alex deliberately shifted closer, letting his shoulder skim hers, feeling the flushed dampness of her skin. “Wild. Amazing that anybody ever managed to get a boat through it...talk about determination."

"It's fantastic," she agreed, surveying the chaos below. "I haven't been here for ages. I'm glad we came."

She shot him a sideways look and a jolt of desire sizzled through him. "Always happy to oblige." He gestured to the stairs. "Ready for the last haul?"

She wiped sweat off her forehead before heading down the treads ahead of him. "I can't believe it's this hot already. It's not even really summer yet. If I can find a nice calm pool, I'm going for a wade."

A few minutes more saw them safely to the river's edge. There was no such thing as a picnic area in this park. They tossed their packs on a flat rock, and began to explore. One of the original winches used for the stern wheelers was still in place—rusty and corroded, but a testament to the will and endeavour of those who chose to settle in Northern British Columbia. He chuckled as June gave it an encouraging pat.

The main channel of the river swept by at a furious rate. But here and there small backwashes swirled, trapped among the rocks. Squatting down next to one, she unlaced her boots and drew off her socks, wiggling her toes.

"Are you going to join me?" She swished a hand in the gently moving water and gasped. "Oh, my, that's freezing!"

"Think I'm scared of a little cold?" he laughed, sitting next to her.

They plunged their bare feet in. He had to suppress a girlish shriek as ice instantly seeped into his bones.

June had no such concern, and squealed loudly. "Good grief! It's worse than I thought!"

He grinned and dipped in his hands, scooping water up his forearms, washing away the sweat of the hike. "Refreshing, isn't it?"

"Sure," she agreed dryly, "although I was thinking more along the lines of bone-numbing."

"You're cranky because you're too hot. Here, let me cool you off." And without other warning, he doused her with a double handful.

She whooped in shock, frantically plucking the saturated fabric off her body. Alex couldn't ignore the way the material clung to the slight curve of her breasts, but kept his gaze on her face, waiting expectantly. She stood up, cloudy brown water swirling around her knees, and took a couple of steps deeper into the pool.

"Oh, that's how you want to play, is it?" she said, dangerously sweet—then paddled swiftly with both hands, sending a solid shower toward him.

He sprang up, face turned from her attack, and dove forward, catching her around the waist and driving her backward. She struggled, flailing strong, lithe arms and legs as he kept a firm grip on her hips. He reversed their positions so she was sitting on his lap, facing him, her knees snugly straddling his thighs. She was soaked and shivering but giggling.

She seized his ears and waggled his head. "You'd better let me up so I can dry off, before I turn into an icicle."

Water darkened her hair to golden wheat and ran in rivulets down her cheeks. It had started in play, but now a craving filled Alex. He knew he should stop torturing himself with her nearness, choke off the urge to touch her, touch her everywhere. Especially if he couldn't give her what she'd asked for, what she deserved. But he was unable to resist.

He reached up and took hold of her hands, drawing them down, clasping them between their bodies. Her face was so near he could see a rim of darker blue surrounding the brilliance of her irises.

He closed the distance until his lips brushed hers. He sucked her bottom lip into his mouth, tasted the faint earthiness of the river and a hint of salt. The suppleness of her buttocks resting on his thighs, her softness pressing against his chest, thrilled him. It was an odd yet glorious sensation, the chilliness of the water and the heat of her body, the warm sun on his shoulders and her cool lips on his. He wrapped his hands in her ponytail and tugged her head back, then traced open mouth kisses down her neck to her collarbone. A deep shudder shook her.

His thoughts clouded over, as silty with sensation as the water swirling around them was silted with sand. She strained her centre against his hardness and bent her head to sketch the whorls of his ear with her tongue. His hands slid down her back to her ass, lifting her, cradling her against him.

He couldn't get enough of how her body demanded, her lips moved, her tongue darted. She purred deep in her throat as he discovered new delights along the length of her neck, behind her ear. She anchored herself in his lap and the little blood remaining in his brain drained out.

With his last coherent thought, he pushed her away, lifting her onto the rock at the edge of the pool, dragging his hands off her body. If he touched her one second longer he would have to have her, and nothing would stop him. His arousal was almost painful. His breath heaved, and it took all his resolve to keep his hands clenched at his side when they burned to touch her.

Her blue eyes were dreamy, heavy with passion.

“We have to stop.” He bit out the words. “I won’t be responsible for what happens next if we don’t stop right now.”

The intensity drained from her face, leaving it wan and still. “How very noble of you, to sacrifice your needs for mine,” she said coldly. “I didn’t ask you to kiss me, but if I hadn’t wanted you to, it wouldn’t have happened. I want you,” she continued bitterly. “It still doesn’t mean I’m ready to sleep with you.”

“What do you want from me?” Frustrated hunger blazed into flame again, but he kept it firmly under control. “What kind of promises? Are you worried I’ll be having sex with someone else if we’re sleeping together? What kind of guy do you think I am?”

He surged out of the pool and stomped a few feet away. Water coursed off the heavy fabric of his shorts and down his calves. He pulled off his shirt and wrung it out.

“I think you’re a very good man,” she said simply. He gathered himself before turning toward her. Hurt was evident in the hunch of her shoulders, the set of her mouth. “And I think you’re mad because you know I’m right.” She got to her feet and stepped out of the pool, but did not approach him. “I don’t want to mess this up. I want to be sure. I want you to be sure.”

Alex thought of his father’s recent announcement, and realized he was ashamed to mention it to June. “Tell me the truth. Tell me straight. Do you believe in marriage? In vows of ‘’til death do us part’?”

She answered without hesitation. “Yes, I do. I

believe there's nothing better than spending your life with someone you love. But I'm not stupid. I know it's not all rainbows and roses. It's hard work. And sometimes, even hard work isn't enough."

He wondered if she was thinking of his parents. She might be willing to give them the benefit of the doubt, but he'd been there, he'd seen it. He wasn't willing to give them even that much.

"I want kids, too." She studied the river rushing past. "And I don't want to put them through the pain of divorce. So I'm going to be very, very careful about who I let into my life. And while I know sex with you would probably be mind-blowing..." she teased a reluctant smile out of him "...having sex will change our relationship. And I want to make sure it changes for the better, not the worse."

He remembered his panic when she'd called for help. Was it really less than two days ago? He could give her that much, at least. "I care about you. It's not only desire, not only sex. It's..." he rolled his shoulders, frustrated at his inability to find the right words. "I don't know what it is. I need to know you're safe, you're happy."

The tension in her arms, her neck, abated. He sighed. "Come on, let's have lunch."

Awkwardness still stuttered as they walked back to where they had dropped their packs. June pulled out a towel and shared it with him.

"Ready to eat?" he asked.

"What did you bring?"

"Let's see." He reached into his pack and pulled out a squashy thermal cooler from which he removed two take out containers, a couple sets of chopsticks, a small bottle of soy sauce, and a bottle of white wine.

June's eyebrows rose. "Sushi? You brought sushi?"

"California rolls, ebi ten, veggie rolls. You like it, right? I'm sure you mentioned it before, when we had dinner together."

"I love it. I can't believe you thought to bring it on a hike."

He handed over a container. "I got it fresh this morning, and it's been in the cooler ever since. Dig in."

Her uneasiness faded, helped along by the hot sun, crisp wine and excellent sushi.

She delicately plucked a slice of pickled ginger with her chopsticks. "Um, I've got a question for you," she said.

"Fire away."

"Maybe this isn't the best time to ask." He gave her a level look. She huffed out a breath and went on. "Fine. When I was at Mom and Dad's, before all the excitement, they invited you to a family dinner on Friday. Feel free to say no if it's too weird, too...whatever." What had recently passed between them fizzed in the air.

He gestured with the wine bottle and she nodded. He topped up her glass. "Who all will be there?"

"Mom and Dad, my younger brother, Zachary. My other brother Sean and his wife and my nephew. I don't think there will be aunts, uncles or cousins, but you never know. There shouldn't be too many of us, though."

Alex snorted at what June considered a small family gathering. "Would this be a kind of test?"

She laughed, a trifle uncertainly. "Probably more for me than you. Remember, you can pick your friends, but you can't pick your family. Once you meet them you might run screaming in the opposite direction, never to think of me again."

He chuckled, pleased at this small show of nerves. Sun glinted off the wine in his glass, turning the pale liquid amber. "Why not? All right, I'll come."

They packed up their debris, then stretched out on the rocks to let the sun finish its job of drying their clothes.

"I think we should stay here forever." He relaxed on his back with his head cushioned on his crossed arms.

"What time is it?" she murmured sleepily, face turned to the sun, leaning on her elbows.

"We don't have to hurry. Come here." He patted his chest. She slid next to him, her head on his shoulder, and rested her arm on his stomach. This, too, was a kind of test. He lay for a long while with June nestled next to him, listening to the peace of the rushing water, the occasional call of a raven, the buzz of a clumsy bumblebee, the rise and fall of her breathing. The sun burned patterns on the inside of his eyelids. His fingers played with the strands of her hair. She was so still, so quiet, she might have fallen asleep.

With great reluctance he nudged her. "I suppose we should get going."

She groaned, then raised her head. They lazily set about collecting their gear for the return trip.

Chapter Ten

"I know it's your day off," June said as they reached the top of the stairs and headed back along the trail, "so maybe you don't want to talk about work. But I was wondering how the meeting went, the one Iain organized."

Alex paused to let her catch up, then took her hand.

"We spent a fair bit of time mapping out the kill sites, and discovered there certainly seems to have been an increase in the McGregor area. Odds are the more there are, the more we'll find, even if we aren't aware of them all. For right now, we're kind of on hold until new evidence shows up...which, unfortunately, means we have to wait for a new kill."

As usual, the return trip seemed a lot shorter than heading out, and in no time at all, they were back at the car park. Just as Alex was making a right hand turn onto the road, his cell phone rang.

"Crap." He dug the phone out of his pocket as he manoeuvred to the narrow shoulder. "It's the office. I'd better take it."

"No problem," June said.

He set the parking brake. "Alex here." His body tightened with stressful awareness, eyes focused inward, all attention on what he was hearing. His side of the conversation was brief and abrupt, flat toned questions.

"Where?"

"Who found him?"

"How long?"

"When will the flight get in?"

"I'll meet them at the hangar."

He lowered the phone, rested his hands on his thighs and continued to stare straight ahead unseeingly.

"Alex?" She reached out her hand, but drew it back before she touched him. "What's happened?"

"Iain Provost found another kill site this morning."

"That's good, isn't it, in a bad way?"

"When the radio room didn't hear from him after his initial report, they tried to contact him, but couldn't. About three hours ago they sent out the 'copter. They found the kill site, and Iain."

"Alex." Alarm crept through her veins. "Tell me. What happened?"

"They found Iain, next to the grizzly. He'd been shot." Alex turned blind eyes toward her. "He's dead."

****

June stayed with Alex for the rest of that dreadful day. By the end of it she was emotionally exhausted and feeling physically frail.

After his shocking announcement, they sat in silence, too stunned to know what to do next. Alex's hand trembled in her grasp.

"I need to be there when they bring him in." His eyes, fogged with grief and tinged with horror, fluttered from June's face to the dashboard, to the phone he still clutched in his hand, unable to settle. "I need to go to the airport. They're bringing Iain in by helicopter. His," he swallowed, then went on, "body will be taken to the morgue. There'll have to be an autopsy."

She was not letting him drive in his state. No

freaking way. “Let’s switch places. I’ll drive you there.”

“I’m okay.” He gave a horrible facsimile of a smile which in no way touched his eyes.

“No, you’re not,” she said bluntly. “Get out. I’m driving, or you’re not going anywhere.”

He fumbled with the clip of his seat belt and walked around the front of the Jeep as if he wasn’t quite sure where to place his feet. She gripped his arm momentarily as they passed, desperate to offer what small comfort she was able. He brushed by her blindly.

Alex spent the entire drive gazing blank-faced out the windshield. Forty minutes later, she pulled up to the hangar the Ministry rented at the Prince George Airport. Alex unlocked the chain-link gate and they stepped onto the tarmac. The enormous white painted circle with a letter H in its centre waited, deserted. A small group of people stood to the left, close to the gigantic double doors leading into the hangar itself.

An older man, dressed in a conservation officer’s uniform, detached himself from the group and came forward to greet Alex. He was strongly built, with a barrel shaped chest and wide shoulders. His hair was silvery grey, and he wore a luxuriant moustache.

“I’m glad you’re here.” His voice was gruff bass that matched his weathered face. “It’s good that you’re here.”

“What do you know, Nelson?” Alex asked sharply. “Linda told me a bit when she called, but you must know more.” Nelson’s voice shook as he gave them the meagre details. Iain had been on call, so when someone had phoned early that morning to say there was a dead grizzly on Red Mountain—not far from the very first kill site Alex and June had gone to—the dispatcher sent

Iain out. The caller had given very detailed directions, and Iain appeared to find the site easily enough. He had radioed in to confirm his location. And that was the last anyone had spoken to him.

When the silence went on long enough to be worrisome, Linda in the radio room called Nelson and asked to send a helicopter out. Using the GPS coordinates Iain had given, the pilot and another conservation officer, Samantha Cross, had flown to the site and discovered Iain's body along with the bear's ransacked hulk. The RCMP were immediately alerted. Investigators flew out in yet another helicopter. Once the RCMP finished their initial procedures, Iain's body would be brought back.

Nelson, Alex and June drifted over to join the others. These included two uniformed RCMP officers and two more conservation officers who had learned of the tragedy. Alex acknowledged his co-workers with a nod. The female police officer introduced herself and her partner as Constables Weston and Lacavalier, asked for June and Alex's names and contact information and jotted it down in a small notebook.

"I will be alerted when the body has departed from the scene," she announced, indicating a cell phone on her belt. The shiny brown leather bulged with a variety of objects, including a snapped down holster. "It could be some time yet."

"There's a room inside we can use," Nelson said.

Everyone trudged in through a metal door, down a battered, blue corridor into a small room smelling of burnt coffee and airplane fuel. They perched on a variety of metal chairs and torn, stained upholstered furniture squeezed haphazardly into the space.

Then they waited.

Conversation was sporadic throughout the next long, tense hours. June learned the older man was Nelson Manning, the regional manager for the Northern Centre of the Conservation Service, based in Prince George. He made pots of coffee and offered it to others, drinking cup after cup himself.

June flipped through a magazine, published two years earlier, filled with technical aviation articles that might as well have been written in Swahili for all she understood them.

She was wondering if the flight would be delayed because of darkness when Constable Weston's phone rang. Weston answered briskly, her conversation studded mostly with grunts. She disconnected and turned to the watchful group. "They should be arriving in about twenty minutes."

What a relief to stand on the tarmac, out of the stifling mechanical atmosphere. An ambulance was parked outside the fence, and the RCMP officers went over to speak with the paramedics standing next to it. Everyone waited quietly.

Twenty minutes stretched to thirty, to forty. Tension itched along June's nerves. At last, Alex lifted his head from his distracted contemplation of the ground at his feet and turned to the northeast.

Moments later June also heard the distinctive sound of a helicopter in flight. The small aircraft approached, a red stretcher strapped to one of the support struts, and made its landing.

Bending below the still whirling blades, Alex approached the craft. The pilot descended and started working on the straps holding the stretcher in place.

Alex assisted him, and then the two of them, escorted by Conservation Officer Samantha Cross, carried their burden across the tarmac. Inside the thick wire mesh of the stretcher rested a still bundle, zipped into a stout black plastic shroud.

Constables Weston and Lacavalier and the paramedics immediately assumed responsibility for the body. They rolled over a wheeled cot and competently transferred the body from its temporary transport. Alex and Nelson followed them to the ambulance. Before the paramedics collapsed the legs of the stretcher and lifted it out of sight, Alex spoke to Constable Weston. She hesitated, then shrugged. Alex reached forward and pulled down the zipper of the body bag. He stood, head bent, hand resting gently on the covered body. Then he closed the zipper, and stepped away.

The ambulance and police cruiser headed back into town. Alex watched them go. June walked to him and stood at his left shoulder. He looked down at her, the corner of his mouth lifting in a small gesture of acknowledgement. The sun, setting on the far side of the airfield, cast a golden glow.

"Let's go," he said. "There's nothing more to do here."

****

It was dark by the time June pulled into the parking lot of Alex's condominium. When she turned off the ignition, the ticking of the engine seemed unnaturally loud.

"Do you want me to come in?" she asked hesitantly. She hadn't even known where he lived until now, and felt intrusive even making the suggestion. But she couldn't bear to think of him going into his empty house on his own.

"I won't be very good company."

"It doesn't matter." Imagining him dealing with his grief without anyone there made her gut constrict and her arms long to hold him. "I don't think you should be alone."

Inside, Alex folded onto the couch as if his legs no longer had the strength to support him.

"We need a drink," she said. "Where do you keep it?"

"In the kitchen." He leaned back, eyes closed.

She found a bottle of Canadian Club stashed in the awkward-to-reach cupboard above the refrigerator. Cracking a few ice cubes from their plastic tray, she dropped them into two squat glasses and topped them with a good measure, then carried them to the living room. Tucking one leg underneath her, she sank onto the cushion next to Alex. He lay slouched down, long legs stretched out in front of him.

"Here." She nudged his arm with the glass. "My dad swears by this after a long day."

He opened his eyes and reached to take the drink. She let the alcohol linger on her tongue. Its heat seeped through her system, dulling the chill she hadn't been able to shake since hearing of Iain's death. Alex swirled the liquid around, ice clinking, then tossed it back in one gulp and placed the glass on the low table in front of him. He took her free hand in his and gripped it tightly.

"He was a good man. He didn't deserve to die that way."

"How long had you known him?" She swept a lock of hair off his forehead, let her fingers linger behind his ear.

"Ever since I came to Prince George. He was my mentor, the one who showed me the ropes, taught me things you can't learn in school. For God's sake, June, what's going on?" he said softly but fiercely. "How could this happen?"

"Do you think it's possible the poachers came back? That Iain saw them?"

"It doesn't make sense. Why kill him? That simply doesn't happen."

"If this poaching ring is organized enough, bringing in tens, possibly hundreds of thousands of dollars, then it might be worth killing to protect it." She sipped her drink. "No one said anything today about Iain's family. Do they know what's happened?"

"Iain and his wife have been divorced for years. They never had any children. I think she went back East after they split up. They were from the Maritimes. Other than her, I imagine Nelson has next of kin listed on paperwork at the office." His hand tightened on hers. "Thank God that's not my job." He closed his eyes. "I'm exhausted."

Deep lines she had never noticed before creased down the side of his nose, and bruises darkened the skin beneath his eyes. It wasn't only physical exertion that took a toll on a person's body. "This morning seems eons ago," she agreed.

His eyes popped open and he sat up straight. "All our gear. It's still in the Jeep. It needs to be cleaned out."

"I'll get it." She stood and motioned him back. "You stay."

He gave in. "Thanks."

She headed into the night and rooted around in the cab. Hefting one pack over her shoulder, she dragged the other out, slammed the door shut and locked it. She glanced up and down the silent residential street. Alex's condo was a narrow three-story structure in a block of six similar homes. Surrounding the parking lot were three more complexes of the same design. Porch lights were on, but most of the windows were dark. Entering the house, she slipped past Alex, still sprawled on the couch, and took the gear into the kitchen. She discarded the takeout food containers and rinsed out the empty water bottles and left them to dry on the drain board. The damp towel in her pack stank of must and mildew, but there wasn't much she could do about that until she got home.

She returned to the living room. Sometime in the last few minutes Alex had fallen asleep. His breathing was deep and even, the new lines carved into his face less noticeable. His hands lay palm up on his thighs.

Her breath caught in her throat, her heart grew tight. At least in sleep he had an escape from grief and anxiety. She stood behind him, smoothing her hands over his shoulders and laying her cheek on top of his head.

He stirred sleepily and his hands came up to hers as they rested on his chest. "Dozed off there," he mumbled.

"I guess I should go."

He tightened his hold. "Not yet," he said. "Come sit with me for a bit."

She settled next to him on the long couch. "Here." She patted her thigh. "Lay your head." She pressed firmly on his shoulders until he gave in, swinging his legs up and curling onto his side.

"Just for a little while," he muttered.

"For a little while," she agreed. In seconds he was

asleep again, his body limp, the weight of his head solid in her lap.

She soothed herself by rubbing her hand down the line of his body. And that's when she knew. She had slipped into love, without even noticing. What had been simple attraction had deepened silently, insidiously. He moved restlessly, a frown growing. She murmured nothings, huddled protectively over him, and he relaxed once more, sliding deeper into sleep.

She stayed awake late into the night, studying her new revelation from every angle. As certain as she was of her own feelings, she was also certain Alex didn't share them.

Yet.

****

June lifted slowly from the depths of slumber. A voice whispered her name. She opened her eyes. Alex knelt on the floor next to her.

"Morning."

"What time is it?" She struggled up, stretched and yawned. She realized she'd been lying on her side, a blanket draped over her. Alex must have woken in the night and rearranged her, but she didn't remember.

"Eight. Why didn't you go home last night? You couldn't have been comfortable."

She circled her neck to work out a crick.

"It wasn't that bad." She didn't want to admit she hadn't been able to bring herself to disturb him as he'd slept with his head in her lap.

"It's not the first time I've slept on this couch," he admitted, "but it's not the way I envisioned our first night together." He brushed a strand of hair out of her eyes, letting his fingers trail over her cheek and down her neck. Her toes flexed in response. "I have to get to the office."

"Oh, I'm sorry. You want me to go." She made an effort to get up, but Alex held her there with a mock scowl.

"That's not what I meant," he said. "I wanted to say goodbye. And to let you know there's fresh coffee in a thermos on the counter."

"Coffee. Thank God," she said.

Alex kissed her forehead. "Take your time. I'll call you later." His hair, damp from his morning shower, curled slightly at the nape of his neck and he smelled wonderfully of soap and shampoo.

She walked him to the door. "I don't think I said this out loud yesterday, but I'm so sorry about Iain."

He paused with his hand on the knob. "Thank you. I want to get in, see if there's any news."

"Go." She gave him a gentle push.

He kissed her, lightly at first, then with growing passion. She fisted her hands in his shirt, sinking into the caress, reveling in the warmth of his body and mouth. He straightened away, searching her face with serious brown eyes. "I'll call you later," he repeated, and was gone.

****

It was an odd feeling, stepping into Alex's bathroom. She used the same soap he had, the same hand towels. Nowhere near intimate enough to use his toothbrush, she made do with scrubbing paste on her teeth with her finger. She longed for a shower, but when she realized the state of her clothes, considerably disheveled from the romp in the water and then a night on the couch, she decided it wasn't worth it. She had time to run home before heading into the office.

Feeling a bit more human, she made her way to the kitchen, found a mug inside one of the standard issue white melamine cabinets, and poured fragrant brew steaming hot from the stainless steel thermos. Cradling the cup in her hands, she began to explore.

A door next to the refrigerator led to an unfinished basement. The kitchen included a small dining area and an archway led to the living room and front entrance. Alex had done little to personalize his home. Cupboards, paint and flooring were basic whites and neutrals, probably original to the condo's construction. No plants, no brightly coloured pillows, no family photos were in evidence.

Masculine influences were everywhere. A large flat panel TV hugged the wall opposite the brown corduroy couch. Three darkly stained wooden tables sat on either side and in front of the sofa, and a vast collection of CDs and DVDs was stored neatly in a tall slotted cabinet. She browsed through them, finding contemporary and classic rock as well as a number of jazz and orchestral albums. Most of the DVDs were nature documentaries produced by the likes of the BBC and Discovery. She wondered if they were gifts someone had decided were appropriate for a man with Alex's job, or if they were his own purchases.

She hesitated before going up the stairs, but couldn't resist. One of the two rooms on the top floor was obviously an efficient home office, with a desk, computer and shelving. The other was his bedroom.

The bed was large and cozy, neatly made with a fluffy dark blue duvet and crisp white pillowcases. A few discarded clothes were heaped on a chair in the corner of the room, but there were no socks on the floor or piles of dirty laundry. Even in his private space, Alex was obviously a neat soul.

She stood awhile longer, breathing in his scent. Then with a long sigh, decided it was time to face the day.

Chapter Eleven

The day before yesterday, after the police had finished their examination of her truck, it had been towed to a shop for a new tire and to have the windows replaced. A short call confirmed it was ready, so she took a taxi from Alex's condo to retrieve it, and headed home.

It seemed disrespectful on this day to wear her usual jeans and T-shirt. After a much needed shower, June put on crisply pressed linen pants and a satiny forest green blouse and set out to the RiverForce office.

Letting herself in with the key she'd been given earlier in the week, she switched on the light and powered up the computer. As she was waiting for it to come to life, the phone rang.

"Ah, June, you're in today." Richard's voice was vibrant and hearty.

"Yes, Richard. You did get my email telling you I wouldn't be around yesterday, right?"

"Of course, of course. Not a problem. Did you have course work to do?"

"No, I spent the day with a friend."

"That reminds me. I heard on the news this morning a conservation officer was killed yesterday. I certainly hope it wasn't that fellow you introduced me to. Allan, wasn't it?"

She closed her eyes and breathed soundlessly

through her nose. Richard had put into words the very thought she had been avoiding for almost twenty-four hours. “His name is Alex, and no, it wasn’t him. We were together when he got the news. The man killed was one of his colleagues.”

Richard cleared his throat. “He was with you yesterday? Isn’t that lucky.”

She pushed the words past the ball of ice in her throat. “Alex is quite upset, of course, but otherwise he’s fine.”

“It’s terrible, just terrible, what happens in this world sometimes.” June waited through a short silence. Then his voice resumed its normal briskness. “I’m calling because I’ve got an assignment for you. Do you mind stepping over to my office?”

The University of Northern British Columbia had been designed with Canadian winters in mind, and most areas of the institution could be reached without going outside. She walked along the polished concrete corridors and into the Administration Wing, where four stories of offices opened into a vaulted central hall pillared with beautifully constructed wooden beams. Richard’s office was on the second level. June introduced herself to his administrative assistant, an older woman in twinset and pearls, who nodded and waved her through.

This space was a far cry from the poky hole assigned to RiverForce. A wall of plate glass provided a stunning view over the city and as far as the eastern horizon, where the snowy crests of the McGregor Mountain Range loomed cold and remote, even on this sunny spring day. Somewhere in that wild landscape Iain had died a lonely, violent death.

She shook the melancholy from her mind and surveyed the rest of the room. A large executive desk dominated the left side, a medley of papers, folders, books and a laptop scattered over it. Richard was seated at a small round conference table near the window, with yet more papers strewn across its surface.

"Do you see this mess?" He gestured with both hands. "Do you wonder how I ever get any work done?" He offered her a chair next to him and continued without waiting for an answer. "I have got to get these into some semblance of order, and then I'll need your help."

"What are they?" She pulled a few of the sheets closer and leafed through them.

"Scripts of the presentations I've done at conferences I've attended on behalf of RiverForce. I need to have them typed up as a Word doc." He continued to sort and stack the pages into piles.

"Didn't you use that program to write them originally?"

He met her gaze half shamefully. "Yes, I did. But I transferred all my files from my old laptop to a new one. Then I went and had the old hard drive erased so I could donate it to a program which provides low income students with computers." He smoothed a hand over his well-groomed beard, and his eyes twinkled with his normal fervour. "And now I can't seem to find these presentations anywhere. I'm afraid I'm terribly old school. I get along with technology, but we'll never be kindred spirits."

She motioned helplessly at the multitude of papers. "When do you need them by?"

"Do you think you might have it done by the end of next week? I know it's a lot of typing, but it is simply copying."

"Couldn't you scan the pages?"

"I need to be able to make revisions to the scripts. You see, I have four main presentations, depending on the conference. But I mix and match from all of them. And, of course, I need to update them with current information."

He staggered the four stacks of pages, placing them in a low, narrow cardboard box, and handed it to June, who accepted it with an internal groan.

"I guess I'd better get started."

Richard escorted her to the outer office. "Thanks again. I'd ask Sarah here to help," he winked roguishly at his assistant, whose pale cheeks flushed slightly, "but it is, after all, RiverForce business."

"No problem. I'll get right on it."

Back in her dim little room, where the nicest view was a poster of Jasper's Maligne Lake tacked crookedly to the wall, she dumped the box on her desk. She'd left her cell phone there, and when she checked for messages, found a text from Alex.

No news re Iain. Are you at work?

She typed back. *Yes. Was in a meeting. Call me.*

While she waited, she retrieved the first pile of pages from the box. Richard was right. It wouldn't be too hard, but it certainly seemed like an excruciating waste of time. With a resigned shrug, she put fingers to the keyboard.

Five minutes later her cell rang.

Alex's voice was low and tired. "It's crazy here. People are walking around like they've been tazered, and the police are all over the place."

She swivelled away from the monitor, opened the

bottom drawer of the desk, and rested her feet on it. “Shouldn’t they be out where Iain was killed?”

“I guess there’s another team out there. The ones here are asking for everybody’s whereabouts yesterday. You might get a call.”

“What about the two officers at the airport? Didn’t they report we came in together?”

“It doesn’t seem to matter. They keep asking the same questions again and again. Then they asked for a list of poachers known to be in the area.”

“Do you have such a thing?”

“We have a list of past offenders, of course. But whether they’ve been out in that area recently, we don’t have a clue. Wait a sec.” Rustling sounds filled the speaker, as if Alex was holding the phone against his shirt, and she heard muffled conversation. He came back on the line. “I’ve got to go. Will I see you tonight?”

“Are you sure? You sound exhausted. Maybe I should stay home.”

“Please, June.” She sensed tightly held emotions bleeding from the simple words. “I need to be with you, even if for only a little while.”

A thrill rippled through her, tinged with guilt. Was she taking advantage of Alex’s distress? She searched her mind for anything she could do to help. “How about I bring dinner to your place? Around six?”

“I would really, really like that.”

She disconnected and turned back to the computer. With a soft oath, she bent to her task.

****

It was early afternoon when June left the office and walked through the sunshine to where she’d parked. As she neared her truck she noticed a piece of paper fluttering against the windshield. She hurried forward, righteous indignation building, ready to wave her receipt under someone's nose and demand they retract the ticket. Ripping the slip from under the wiper blade, she realized it was an unremarkable sheet of office paper. She unfolded it. Her confusion curdled into horror.

Tell your boyfriend to stay out of the mountains unless he wants to end up like his buddy.

Ice trickled down her spine. She read the chilling words again. A couple of students walked past, complaining about an assignment, and the spell was broken. She threw herself into the truck, fumbling the key into the ignition. Tires spun as she raced out of the lot.

****

June arrived in a flurry at the Ministry of Environment building. The man staffing the front desk had a scrawny neck, a large blemish on his high forehead, and glazed eyes. Breathlessly, she asked him to call Alex. He stared at her blankly before answering.

"I'm sorry. All conservation officers are unavailable today. Would you like to leave a message?"

"No. No, I need to see him. It's about Iain Prevost."

That made him pick up the phone, and moments later Alex was striding down the corridor toward her.

"What's going on?"

She clutched his outstretched hand in both of hers. "I have something to show you. Can we go to your office?"

Once inside, she shut the door and pulled the sheet of paper out of her bag. "Here."

Alex leaned a hip against the desk and read the short sentence, a frown creased between his eyebrows.

"Where did you get this?"

"It was tucked under the wipers on my truck when I left work this afternoon."

He was silent, studying the note.

"We have to show this to the police," she said.

"Of course we do," he replied absently. "Just give me a minute."

"This is a threat." Panic bubbled. She did her best to keep her voice calm and level, but Alex's attention lifted from the paper. "Whoever wrote this is threatening to kill you."

Whatever he saw in her face made him open his arms. "Come here." She slipped into his embrace, nestling her nose into the hollow at the base of his throat. She took a deep breath, and then another. Her pulse settled for the first time since she'd read the message.

"Okay, I'm better now." But she stayed where she was, breathing in his scent, spicy and male. His hands slid up and down her back. His lips caressed her temple.

He tipped her face up with a finger on her chin. "Let's go find the investigators." He pressed his mouth briefly but firmly to hers before guiding her to the door.

****

The RCMP investigation had commandeered one of the boardrooms on the second floor of the building. Inside were two senior officers, as evidenced by their plain clothes, and, to June's surprise, a uniformed Constable Wendy Hoffarth as well.

The brusque blonde who had taken her statement the day after the motorcycle attack approached June as Alex strode toward the seated men.

"What are you doing here?" Hoffarth asked curtly.

"I found something." June focused on Alex as he slid the paper across the dark surface of the table.

"What?"

"A death threat."

Hoffarth started, then stepped to the table and peered surreptitiously over the shoulders of her superiors. June followed, taking a place next to Alex.

Both investigators wore business suits but no ties. One of them sported grey hair, cut severely short, grey eyes to match and a five o'clock shadow about three hours early. Using the end of a pen, he slipped the note into a clear evidence bag and sealed it shut. He read in silence, then passed it to his colleague.

This officer was younger, with coal black hair, dark skin and a prominent nose. "Who has handled this paper?" he asked.

"I did, of course," June said, "and Alex, but no one else."

"Tell me about it," the older officer said.

She did so.

"You were with Mr. Weaver when he investigated two recent poaching sites, were you not?"

"Yes, I was." No one introduced either of the men, but their authority was clear. "I was also with Alex all day yesterday, from about nine in the morning. When was Iain Prevost killed?"

An internal debate was conducted behind the careful grey eyes. Her question was answered grudgingly. "The coroner puts it between ten a.m. and noon." He turned his attention to Alex. "Do you have any idea who might have reason to threaten you? Someone who knows both you and Ms. Brandt?"

Alex shook his head. "No one."

June offered up the last slim hope she still clutched. "Are you sure it wasn't an accident? Is there any chance Iain wasn't killed...on purpose?"

"No weapon was found in the vicinity of Mr. Prevost's body, which appears to rule out suicide." Alex hissed air between his teeth. "An accident is still possible, but if so, the shooter has not approached police."

"Iain didn't kill himself." Fury burned in Alex's voice. "He was murdered."

The ominous word punched June in the stomach.

"It's always best to keep an open mind during any investigation," the older officer said. "But the evidence tends to agree with you. Especially with this." He gestured to the note.

Constable Hoffarth spoke up. "Ms. Brandt was also involved in a hit and run with a motorcyclist." She summed up June's statement succinctly. All three of the RCMP members studied June, their faces revealing nothing.

"This incident also took place at the university," stated the dark-haired man.

June nodded. "There's something else. Maybe you already know, but I was shot at a couple of days ago." She filled in the details. Her fingers twisted together, hidden in her lap. It was getting harder and harder to convince herself these events were isolated episodes. Could she really, truly be in grave danger? She and Alex?

Both investigators asked a number of questions, all of which she had attempted to answer more than once in the previous days. She still had no idea what anything meant, who could be behind it.

"We'll need the details on your truck." June gave them. Constable Hoffarth noted them down. "And your fingerprints. Both of you."

Hoffarth snapped open a silvery metal case, pulled out the necessary equipment and motioned June forward. She cleaned June's fingertips with a ready wipe, rolled each of them on the ink-pad and then the form. She handed her tissues to clean up with, then repeated the process with Alex. No one spoke.

"Thank you," the older officer said neutrally. "You can go now."

****

Alex did his best to appear calm, but he couldn't ignore the feeling of standing on the edge of a precipice, struggling for balance.

He and June had returned to his office. "What do you think they're going to do now?" she asked.

He gave what he hoped was a nonchalant shrug. "Check for fingerprints, ask around to find out if anyone was seen near your truck."

June pulled her ponytail over her shoulder and sleeked it restlessly between her fingers. "I don't imagine there's much of a chance they'll discover anything."

"That would be farfetched, I think. The security guards aren't there all the time, they only make the rounds. It would be simple enough to do with no one noticing. And even if they were seen, who would care? Half the time I park up there someone's tucking advertisement flyers under wiper blades."

In the depths of June's large shoulder bag her cell phone rang. She fished it out and frowned at the display. "Do you mind?" Alex beckoned her to go ahead.

"Hello?"

"Oh, my God, June, I heard on the news! It's not your game warden, is it? He's not the one, is he?" The woman's voice was loud enough for even Alex to hear.

June winced but replied sedately, "No, Tabitha, it's not." She moved to the tall narrow window, and he could no longer hear what the caller was saying.

After listening for a while, June spoke. "It's okay, really. We're fine." She smiled faintly over her shoulder at Alex. "I'm kind of busy right now, Tabitha. Was there anything else? Sounds good. Okay. Bye."

She tossed the phone back in her bag. "Sorry about that."

"Friend of yours?"

"Tabitha Scala. Someone I know from RiverForce. We're not friends so much as meeting buddies...you know, the person you end up sitting next to all the time. She heard about Iain's...what happened to Iain. Underneath all the drama I'm sure she's genuinely concerned, but it's not real to her. I only met Iain once, and even I can't really take it in."

Alex dropped into his chair and scrubbed his eyes with the heels of his hands, avoiding the sympathy on her face. "I don't know when the funeral is going to be. Iain's ex-wife asked the Ministry to organize everything. She's not coming back."

"It's hard for you, I know. For everyone in the office, I'm sure."

He lifted his head. Her lips were bloodless, her eyes glistening with unshed tears. He rose and went to her. "Are you okay? What's going on in that brain of yours?" He tapped her forehead gently with one finger, let it ride down the bridge of her nose to caress her mouth, before resting his hands on her shoulders.

The words came boiling out. “That note, Alex. How can you be so calm? It was a death threat...directed at you.”

Startled by her forcefulness, he attempted to soothe her. “Sticks and stones. Words can’t hurt me.”

“But what if it’s not just words? What if *you* were supposed to get the tip yesterday? If someone wanted to lure you out where they could hurt you, what better way? You were supposed to be on call, remember. You switched with Iain.”

The skin on his jaw prickled and sweat sprang on his upper lip. He gripped her arms.

“Good God,” he whispered. “It’s my fault.”

“No!” she said urgently. “No, that’s not what I meant. Listen to me, Alex.” She broke free of his grasp and raised her hands to his cheeks, forcing him to meet her eyes. “It’s not your fault. The person to blame is the one who killed Iain. But you have to see...you have to realize...it could have been you. And the note...maybe it was supposed to be you.”

He fought back the dizziness threatening to engulf him, struggled to concentrate on her words through the roaring in his ears.

“You have to be careful. You have to take care. Because it can’t happen...I can’t lose you.” She repeated it. “I can’t lose you. Not now. Not ever.”

Her brilliant blue gaze held fire and courage and something else he was afraid to define. He wrapped his arms around her and held on, drawing strength from her warmth, her slender softness. That he might have unwittingly been the means of Iain’s death shook him to his core. Years of friendship and respect, blasted away by a bullet. He wasn't sure he could bear the guilt.

"Come to me." He murmured in her ear. "Come to me tonight." His mouth seared a hot, moist path along her jawline. He needed her, but he realized with wonder it wasn't simply sexual. It was also the desire for comfort and companionship, a sharing of sorrow.

The uneasiness icing his veins was consumed in the flame of passion. Unable to deny himself another taste of her, his lips met hers fiercely, grinding against her teeth until her mouth opened and their tongues twisted together, twirling, teasing. He crushed her against his body, hands sliding from buttocks to shoulders, melding her to fit him. "I need you, June." Desperation filled him, undeniable and indefensible. "It's your call. Your decision. But I want you so bad. I..." he faded to a stop, pressed his mouth to hers once more. "Come to me."

Her breath trembled out. He held her so close he could see his reflection in her eyes. She nodded. "Tonight."

Chapter Twelve

Alex paced from living room to kitchen, glaring at the clock. He was as randy as a teenager, as nervous as a boy planning to get to second base, instead of a grown man waiting for a woman he admired, respected and desired. They were both adults, he argued with himself, both able to make their own decisions. If June hadn't wanted to come tonight, she could have said so. Would have said so. But when he remembered his actions in the office earlier, he flinched. He'd needed her, and still did, but had he come on too strong, been too insistent? She had told him she wanted a commitment. She had asked for more time to see where they were going together. And then he had practically begged her to sleep with him tonight. He scraped a hand across his chin, irritated with himself.

The doorbell rang.

June stood on the step, shifting the paper bag she carried from one arm to the other. She flicked a glance at him, not meeting his eyes. The sensations in his stomach had nothing to do with the delicious scent of Chinese takeout wafting in.

"Here, let me take that." He reached for the bag, and when his fingers brushed hers she jumped like she'd been zapped with static. He pretended not to notice, and led her to the tiny dining nook.

A bottle of wine waited, uncorked, next to two thin

stemmed glasses with elegantly wide bowls. Tall tapered candles shone with a steady glow. A single rose lay across one plate. She delicately caressed a velvety red petal.

"I know, it's cliché. But I thought...I wanted..."

He couldn't avoid her eyes, and heat swept up his neck.

Damn it, he was not blushing. He never blushed. He rolled his shoulders to relieve the tightness in his muscles. "I wanted to give you...something."

She lifted the rose off the plate and brought it to her lips, his eyes following the movement. He swallowed. "I need to say something. About this afternoon. I think I might have pressured you." He wished she would speak, but she only stared at him with those deep blue eyes, the rose near her mouth. "I don't want you to feel like that. If you're not ready, say so and..."

She slid the silky blossom against his lips, and he stopped.

"Thank you," she said, and replaced the rose with her mouth.

****

When he'd asked her to come to him, the love she'd discovered in herself such a short time ago had coursed through her, and she'd realized in an odd tangle of despair and delight there was very little she would deny him. Her will crumbled against the torrent of his need. To hear him, now, offering to deny that need, made her love him even more.

The strength of his desire radiated out from him and she absorbed it readily as they clung together. It soaked into every fibre of her being, flickered deep into her centre. She wrapped her arms around his neck, winding her fingers into soft, glossy hair. His mouth opened under hers, and wet wildness seethed between them. His hands gripped her waist, hauling her hard against his body, and she arched against him, purring deep in her throat.

He answered with a growling groan, dragging his lips from hers and trailing them down her neck. She shivered ecstatically as he licked along her collar bone, curving back in his arms to give him greater access. His hand came up, cupping her breast, taunting the nipple with his thumb.

They shuddered together. A fine vibration ran through his body, like a plucked guitar string. Sinking against him for support and sensation, she reached with unsteady fingers for the buttons of her shirt.

Alex's eyes, glazed with greed, watched steadily. His hands slid up her ribs, slipping the blouse from her shoulders, finding their way to the clasp at the front of her bra. So gently, so slowly, he peeled back the lace. Cool air pebbled her naked skin, replaced by fire wherever his gaze travelled.

"Beautiful," he whispered. "God, so beautiful." He dipped his head to her breast.

The shock of it sent a thrill through to her core. She gasped, grasping his shoulders. He drew the nub taut into his mouth, laving it with his tongue, and she lost all sense of self. When he pulled away, she whimpered and stretched up, wordlessly begging for more.

He laughed, a catch in his breathing betraying the fact he was far from unmoved himself. "We're supposed to have dinner, first."

She wiggled against him, feeling his hardness through his jeans. "I'm not hungry." She nibbled his bottom lip.

"Oh, God," he moaned. "Wait, just wait." He backed away, taking her hand and staggering for the stairs, dragging her behind. "At least until we get to the bedroom."

They fell onto the cool blue comforter, a hot tangle of limbs and lips and lust. June slid her hands under his cotton T-shirt, palms pressed to the firm flesh of his chest, skimming through the wiry hairs. She circled the raised bud of his nipple with a fingernail and he sucked in a sharp breath.

"Take your shirt off. Please," she said shakily.

He pulled it over his head. Her hands savoured his body, as if she no longer controlled them, as if they belonged to someone else. She traced the line of dark hair, following it as it arrowed down and disappeared into his jeans. Her fingertips grazed the waistband, brushing against the bones of his hips.

He grabbed her hands and pinned them on the mattress over her head. "You're killing me." He kissed her roughly, tongue and teeth demanding. "But I can't get enough of you."

His breath fluttered along her cheek. He tasted of coffee and mint.

They explored each other thirstily, thoroughly, half-dressed but completely aroused. The blood coursed thickly through her. His fingers dallied over her belly to the fastening of her slacks and stopped. She sighed in protest and raised her hips, inviting him, begging him.

His eyes were black with hunger. "I can still stop," he said, voice hoarse. "If you say it, I'll stop now. God, don't say it."

She was fluid, liquid, boneless. "Touch me. Please,

touch me."

He fumbled slightly as he undid the button and zipper, then slid the material down her thighs, over her knees, and swept it away. She lay helpless, watching him, feeling his eyes trail up her legs, resting for a breathless instant where a tiny scrap of flimsy lace pretended to hide her private self, lifting to her breasts, to her face. He lowered himself alongside her, resting on his elbow. With his fingertips he blazed glory along the inside of her arm, on the underside of her breast, over her navel, along the muscle of her thigh. She quivered, and instinctively her legs opened, exposing her centre to his questing hand.

His touch through the thin material sent a rush of excitement pouring through her. He stroked, unhurried but relentless, until her breathing was ragged and panting. Kaleidoscopes flashed behind her eyelids. Earthquakes of sensation flooded through her, taking her higher and higher, until release rippled violently out to every cell in her body.

When cool air replaced the heat of Alex's body she forced her eyelids open. He stood next to the bed, removing the rest of his clothing. Strength returned to her limbs at the sight of his arousal.

Slowly he stretched himself above her. She reached around to cup his buttocks, feeling him hard and hot against her. The hairs of his chest chafed her breasts erotically.

"Open for me," he said. She shifted slightly, and in a slick, smooth motion they were joined.

She closed her eyes, basking in how he filled her.

"Look at me," he commanded. "I want to see your eyes as I take you."

She clung to him, letting him ride, meeting him stroke for stroke. His hot brown eyes bore into her. She struggled to stay present, but was swamped in a rush of feeling that had her going blind and stiffening against him. He thrust deep, holding himself still at the peak of his release, then collapsed on top of her.

Revelling in the weight of his body pressing down on her, June let her arms fall lethargically from his back and stretched sexily. She felt replete, satiated—and as if she might burst with love. But she bit her lip, holding back the words she was sure would send him running out of her life.

Alex rolled to his side and curled around her back, tucking his knees behind hers, extending the intense connection they had shared. He nuzzled her ear, making her giggle.

"That didn't go exactly as I had planned."

Anxiety speared through her. "What do you mean? I thought it went darn well."

He tap-danced his fingertips over her ribs, making her squirm. "We were supposed to eat first. I'm starving."

She relaxed again and smacked his wandering hand. "Now you mention it, me, too. Do you like cold Chinese food?"

"Love it."

"Can we eat it in bed?"

"As long as you promise to stay naked."

He surprised another laugh out of her, and she twisted in his arms so they were nose to nose. "I will if you will."

"You're on."

****

"Come on, Bee, let's go for a ride." June lifted the toddler into her arms and spun around, her hair flying free, her short, breezy skirt flirting with legs beginning to tan. The boy, a round-cheeked rascal with flyaway dark hair and the devil in his eyes, who obviously had his aunt well wrapped around his sticky little fingers, shouted for more. Alex watched the woman and boy spin and tumble. He had never seen anything so heart-stopping in all his life. He also mused on how to convince June to wear skirts more often. And when he would next have those long, shapely legs bound around him.

June snuggled the little boy in her arms and rubbed her cheek against his, making the child bubble with glee. Alex was shocked by a powerful stab of longing. Was this a true glimpse of the life they might have together? She wanted marriage, children—she'd been clear on that from the start. He was swept up, swamped by all the tomorrows he didn't believe in, hadn't believed possible. A hard ball stuck in his throat. Nerves skittered through his gut.

They had arrived to find the house and yard buzzing with activity. The crowd eventually sorted itself out into June's oldest brother, Sean, his wife, Hillary, and their three-year-old son, Brian; June's younger brother, Zachary, and a couple of his friends; an aunt and uncle and another middle aged couple who might have been neighbours. Introductions had been fast and loud and he was hoping there wouldn't be a quiz.

If meeting so many people at once hadn't befuddled him, the house certainly had. His previous visit had been so fraught with worry for June that he hadn't even noticed its dotted exterior and unusual design. He finally decided only jaded, stiff-neck snobs wouldn't enjoy its fun and originality.

Shortly after his arrival, he'd been embarrassed yet amused when June's parents each pulled him aside privately to thank him for bringing June to them the night of the shooting. Monica pecked his cheek with a light kiss and did her best to hide her worry. Karl shook his hand and regarded Alex with a look both grateful and guarded.

Laughing, June set her nephew down and let him scramble off to plague a long-suffering but ever patient Bauer. She snagged a beer from the cooler outside the back door and flopped into a lawn chair next to Alex, twisting off the cap and taking a long drink. She chuckled as Zach was tackled in the friendly but ferocious football game going on in the large grassy area beside the house.

"Whew, it's hot!" She took another gulp. "It's hard to believe it's not even the end of May."

"It's been a dry spring." Alex sipped his own beer, enjoying the acrid coolness. "The Ministry is worried about a bad forest fire season."

Karl presided over the barbeque, ignoring the instructions of his oldest son about whether or not to use barbeque sauce on the steaks. Sean was a bit taller than his sister, but dark-haired and eyed, like their father. His wife was a cheerful redhead taking motherhood in stride, responding calmly and easily to the demands of her son. She and Monica made numerous trips from the kitchen to the picnic table set up under the shade of a large cottonwood tree. They brought out more food than a platoon would need, Alex decided. All this happy domesticity made him a bit twitchy.

June nudged his knee with her sandaled foot. “You’re kind of quiet,” she said softly. “Anything wrong?”

He shrugged, took another sip from the long necked bottle. “I’m fine.” She gave him a bright blue “oh really” glare. “Okay, I’m a bit antsy. I’m not used to big families.” His own parents had never given him the opportunity to experience the bonds he sensed in June’s family.

She drawled, “You ain’t seen nothing’ yet. We’re breaking you in easy. But it’s more than that,” she added. “You’ve been quiet since you picked me up. Has there been news about Iain?”

He was uneasy at being read so clearly. “The autopsy report and firearms test results came in,” he said. “The bullets that killed the bear and Iain match. And as the poachers would have had to wait around for hours, since the tip was obviously called in after they shot the bear, it certainly looks like Iain was lured out there to be killed.”

Goose bumps rippled on her arms, despite the sultry sun. She opened her mouth to speak, but right then Monica shouted out, inviting everyone to dish up. Hungry people hurried for the table. With a lopsided grin, June offered Alex her hand and they joined the rush.

They filled their plates, then settled on the springy green grass, leaving places at the table for the older generation.

Sean dropped next to June. In a practised move, he tucked Brian onto his lap, and began helping his son eat.

“So, Alex, how’d you hook up with my sister?” he asked, deftly catching the sippy cup Brian was attempting to throw across the lawn and distracting him with a spoonful of baked potato.

"Hook up." June snorted. "Classy, Sean."

"Hey, I'm asking for general info." Her big brother smirked. "I don't need the dirty details."

"That's lucky," Alex said. He was surprised at how effortless it was to take part in the bantering. "Because you're not getting any."

They chatted as they ate. Brian scooted off when he was finished, and the three adults were left lounging on the lawn.

"Are you still involved in that RiverForce group?" Sean asked June.

She nodded. "I'm working for them this summer, doing grunt work in the office."

"What's the name of the guy that runs it? Richard something or other?"

"Fleetham."

"Curly hair, beard, not too tall?"

"Sounds like him."

"Huh." He lapsed into silence, sipping his beer.

She gave his shoulder a friendly punch. "Why are you asking?"

"I was out McGregor way a few weeks ago, four-wheeling with the guys, and I think I saw him. He and this big fellow were getting out of a trucked parked on an old logging road. I knew he seemed familiar—I've seen him on the news a few times—but I couldn't put my finger on it until now. Your ugly face reminded me."

June stuck out her tongue.

Something about Sean's story sent unease twinging along Alex's nerves. "When was this?" he asked.

"Beginning of May. I remember because it was the

day after Hillary's birthday. I took her out to a swank restaurant Friday, then the next day went out with the guys."

Alex's eyes met June's. "The weekend before we met at Longworth."

Puzzlement creased her forehead. "Sounds like it." She turned to Sean. "You sure it was Richard?"

"Of course not. But I remembered it, because they acted kind of weird. See, us guys were taking a break down by the river, and I'd lost the toss to get more beer, so I climbed up the bank back to the road. There's a bend there, and these two dudes had parked before it, so they wouldn't have seen our truck further around the corner. I didn't get a good look, but when I saw the first guy I thought he was carrying a gun, some big mother of a rifle. When they saw me pop out of the bush they got back in the truck right away and drove off." He belched into his fist. "Excuse me. Seemed kind of odd, you know what I mean?"

June shook her head. "It couldn't have been Richard. I'm sure he was in Vancouver at a conference then. The records are in the River Force office."

Sean shrugged. "Like I said, I thought he was familiar, but it might not have been him." Just then, Brian let out a shriek as he tumbled off the low step at the back door. Sean jumped up to console the sobbing boy.

June and Alex helped clean up the remains of the meal, then made their excuses.

Monica walked with them to the Jeep. "I hope you enjoyed yourself, Alex. I'm sorry we didn't get more of a chance to chat."

"That's all right, Mrs. Brandt."

June's mother waved off the formality. "Call me Monica. I also wanted to give my condolences. It's an awful thing about your colleague. Karl and I have been following the story in the news."

"It's been a tough week for us all." Alex opened the door for June and she slid in, then he walked around to the driver's side. "Thank you for dinner. I had a good time."

"You're welcome." Monica smiled. "Come back soon."

****

Alex pulled up in front of June's house. The late spring day was beginning to fade, and the slanting rays of the dying sun painted the trees overarching the street with caramel. He caressed her knuckles with his thumb and brought her hand to his lips. A wonderful lethargy stirred through her.

"Come in with me?" she asked.

He gave her a steady stare from under his brows, dark hair falling into his eyes, sharp cheekbones highlighted by the evening light slipping through the windshield. He lipped her finger, drawing the tip into his mouth and circling it with his tongue. She wanted that mouth. Wanted it everywhere. On her lips, on her breasts, on her body.

"Please," she whispered, "come in with me."

She was in his arms the instant the door closed, straining against him, glorying in a long, deep kiss and the feel of his hands in her hair. She feverishly unbuttoned his shirt and pushed the material off his shoulders, stringing hot, open mouthed kisses across his chest, clasping her arms around his narrow waist.

With a muffled oath he grasped her hips and lifted

her. She wrapped her legs around him. He stumbled to the couch while she clung to him, her butt fitting perfectly between his thighs, her heels pressing against his back. His lips inflamed the skin of her neck. He muttered incoherently as he undid the clasp of her bra, drew it free and feasted on her breasts.

Edgy thrills ripped through her. The knowing of what was happening, the anticipation of all the touches and tastes to come, heightened the sensation, arousing her to new pitches of excitement.

His hands slid up her thighs, under the light material of her skirt and to the thin barrier of her panties. Her breath hitched as his fingers found their way between their bodies and into her hot, moist centre.

They tumbled to the floor, a jumble of arms and legs, avid mouths and eager hands. Shivers raced over her as he lapped his way across her stomach, tongued her navel. And when his mouth touched her aching wetness, she exploded with a ragged scream, arching toward him, trapping him, her legs around his shoulders.

She lay, chest heaving, as she clawed her way back. He discarded his jeans, then lowered himself to her. She reached up with both hands to cup his face. In a moment too sweet for words, she kissed him tenderly. They rocked together, and the waves built, reaching a crescendo surpassing any she had known before.

****

Alex lay, slack-muscled, his face tucked into the curve of June's neck. He considered lifting his weight off her, but her arms held him tightly. Her hair tickled his nose, the citrus scent of her shampoo teasing, tempting.

She stretched under him, scraping her nails down

his back, and arousal flared again. He tamped it down.

"I'll move as soon as I can," he said. "I must be crushing you."

"No hurry. I am, oh, so fine." Her voice was husky and a tad smug. It would have made him laugh if he'd had any energy left.

They crawled back up on the couch and wrapped themselves in a blanket, June's back against Alex's chest. She held his hand tucked under her chin, his leg lay over her thigh. Her breast was silky against his arm as she breathed.

For a long while they were silent, then he shifted to rest his elbow on the arm of the couch. He looked down at her. "We need to talk."

Chapter Thirteen

How could four short words cause such panic? She knew loving Alex might cause her heartbreak. Yet she had allowed herself to hope. And what did it mean, saying those doom-filled words so soon after making love? She replied cautiously. “About what?”

“Did you notice something odd today, at your parents?”

She was bewildered, until she realized he was talking about the investigation, not their relationship. Then his words took on whole new meaning. Her sated, relaxed feeling seeped away. “What Sean said, about seeing Richard?”

“What would an environmental activist be doing with a guy with a rifle, on an old logging road?”

She sat up, the blanket pooling at her waist. The hairs of his chest bristled against her back, oddly comforting. “You know what else is strange? I know Sean didn’t say much about the guy with Richard—if it was Richard—but it reminded me of that night at the restaurant. He was with a big guy then.”

Alex nodded. “I thought of that, too.”

“There’s any number of good reasons for Richard to be out in the back country,” she speculated. “After all, he loves the land, the wildlife. He’s so passionate about it! And even if they did have a gun, it could have been for safety. It’s never smart to go into the bush without protection." She stopped herself when she realized how shrill and desperate she sounded. She breathed in deeply, blew out lightly. "This is all moot, anyway, because I've seen the paperwork. Richard was in Vancouver that weekend."

Alex spoke, his voice as soft as the fingers sweeping through her hair. "I know you admire the man. But be honest. You're thinking what I'm thinking...there's a possibility that Fleetham was in the area the same weekend that grizzly was poached."

She brushed the bangs out of her eyes with a jerky movement. "I can't believe it," she said. "I won't believe it. You don't know what he's like. There's no way Richard could be involved in poaching." The idea made her insides clench. "There's got to be another explanation. I'll have to ask."

"Ask what?" His hand tightened on her shoulder, forcing her to face him. Gone was the gentle understanding. In its place was cold professionalism. "Ask him if he's a criminal? I don't think so."

"I'll be more subtle than that," she said tartly. "All I have to do is ask Richard an innocuous question about his trip to Vancouver. I'll say I need a receipt or something. Then we'll know for sure he couldn't have been on the mountain."

Alex rose from the couch, grabbed his boxers and yanked them on. "June, don't do that. Leave this to me. If I ask the questions, it's coming in an official capacity."

"But that makes it worse! If I ask, Richard won't know we ever thought about it. I'd never be able to look him in the eye again if he discovered we'd ever considered him a poacher. If you ask, he'll know exactly what we're thinking."

He seized her elbows and pulled her to her feet, lifting her up onto her toes. She clutched the blanket around her, feeling foolish and defenceless in her near nakedness.

"Maybe you're right. Maybe Fleetham has nothing to do with the poaching. But if you're wrong, if he is involved, he is also involved in Iain's death." He shook her gently but emphatically. "We're not just talking about a poaching ring. We're talking about murder." She flinched at the word. "Please, don't do anything. Let me take care of it. Or better yet, someone else from the Ministry, or the RCMP. That way, there will be no connection to you at all."

Her icy fingers gripped the blanket between her breasts. "All right," she said, giving in. "I won't talk to him. But you've got to take care of this fast. I can't go into work next week, wondering if I've got a murderer for a boss."

He grazed her forehead with his lips. "I will. I'm going into the office now, get the ball rolling. I'll call you." He quickly finished dressing, gave her an absent-minded kiss, and was gone.

****

Despite their combined efforts, neither the Ministry nor the RCMP was able to track down Richard during the weekend. June spent most of the time making busy work for herself, as even vacuuming and dusting was better than obsessing over what was going on with the investigation.

When she spoke to Alex late on Sunday evening, he sounded tired and frustrated.

"We're all set to do the interview. I talked with

Sean and got the names of his buddies. It took a while for us to get a hold of them, and then they weren't much help. Neither of them had seen anyone, although they did say Sean mentioned seeing the other men when he came back from getting the beer, so there is some confirmation at least. I coordinated with the RCMP, and they've been in touch with the conference organizers in Vancouver. We got lucky there, and found someone in the office even though it's a weekend. But that's where our progress ends. The problem is Fleetham wasn't a guest speaker at the conference, he was a regular delegate, and there was no formal registration after the first day, which was a Wednesday. That gives Fleetham plenty of time to get back to Prince George by the supposed sighting on the weekend. The best way to confirm is to ask Fleetham for the names of people who might have seen him there. And as we can't get a hold of him, we're at an impasse. We've left messages for him everywhere, but he's not getting back to us."

June absently licked her thumb and swabbed at a smudge on the window as she stood, gazing out onto the street. "His schedule's in the system at RiverForce. I suppose I could check it out for you." She felt torn, unwilling to believe Richard was involved, but wanting to find out for sure so the investigation could move on.

"There's no need to do anything tonight. We've done all we can, and without more evidence there isn't much urgency from either the Ministry or the police."

She heard him stifle a yawn, and guilt jabbed her. He was doing his job, was doing what needed to be done to find a criminal, but resentment bubbled in her whenever he spoke of his suspicions.

With a conscious effort, she said warmly, "I'll go in

early tomorrow. If he gets in touch with you before I do, there's no harm done. And if not, maybe I'll be able to help."

"I appreciate it." He went on after a slight pause. "I understand this must be difficult for you. I don't know Fleetham like you do, but the little I've seen of him, on the news and such, I've been impressed. That's why we have to do this, to clear him of any possible involvement. I hope you realize that."

June sighed. "I'm trying to. Honestly, I'm trying to."

After a restless night, she rose early, and was at the RiverForce office well before eight. She resolutely refused to believe Richard had anything to do with a criminal enterprise, but she understood Alex had to follow up any lead, however slight. She powered on the computer and impatiently waited for it to boot up, then called up Richard's schedule on the internal server. She phoned Alex on his cell and caught him as he was leaving home.

"According to his calendar, Richard should be in the office today." She clicked backward through the dates. "It looks like he was here on Thursday—he had a meeting with Thomas, that fellow from RiverForce I told you about before—and he's got a meeting with a couple of grad students at eleven this morning. But it doesn't say anything about where he was this weekend."

"I'll let the office know. If we can't get him on the phone I think we'll send a team to wait for him. How long will you be there?"

"A couple of hours. I'm still retyping Fleetham's speeches, and we're supposed to have our monthly meeting next Sunday night. I need to prepare for that."

"I won't be part of the team interviewing Fleetham, but I'll let you know how it goes. Keep your head down, okay?"

"I will. This is so hard. The waiting, I mean. I want it to be over."

"It will be soon, I promise."

****

June concentrated intently on her work, putting aside any worries about the investigation, and came up for air around ten o'clock, craving a coffee. She bought a latte at the kiosk in the hall and stepped out into the Agora. Sitting against the wall, she basked in the heat reflecting off the stone exterior.

A voice trilled her name, and she turned her head to see all the magnificent glory of Tabitha Scala bearing down. She was resplendent in an emerald green tunic, black leggings and knee-high red leather boots. Her usual assortment of beads and bangles glittered and glimmered around her neck and wrists, and her mane of chestnut hair hung loose over her shoulders. "June!" she repeated delightedly. "How are you?"

It was impossible not to appreciate the sight. "I love your outfit."

Tabitha waved a dismissive hand, bracelets jingling musically. "Are you sure you're all right? You are rather pale."

"It's been a rough few days." And today would likely be no better.

"Of course it has, sweetie. I can't stop thinking about that poor man. And how easily it could have been your fellow! If they hadn't switched their on call days, it might have been him."

"Stop it." June snapped. "A man was killed, was

murdered. Isn't that enough? Do you have to be so...so ghoulish about it?"

Tabitha pressed a be-ringed hand against her breast, a wounded look on her face. "I'm sorry, dear. I didn't mean to upset you."

June took a mental pace back from the edge of her anger. "No, I'm sorry. I shouldn't have shouted at you."

"You know what you need? You need a holiday." Tabitha nodded, immensely pleased at the idea. "You should get out of the city. Where did you go recently? Where you met your young man?"

"Longworth Mountain."

"Yes, Longworth Mountain. You should go back there for a few days."

"You know," June said thoughtfully, "that's an excellent idea."

"If you're going to go, don't delay." Tabitha reached down and patted the top of her head as if she was an obedient puppy. "A few days will do you a world of good, I'm sure." She swooped away in a swirl of musky scent and clinking jewelry.

June headed home shortly after her conversation with Tabitha. Every minute after eleven seemed to last an hour, but a little while before noon her phone rang. She snatched it off the kitchen table.

"He didn't show." Alex's voice was clipped with frustration. "The team was there at ten-forty-five a.m., and they sat and waited along with the grad students he was scheduled to meet. About eleven-fifteen a.m., Richard called his secretary. She told him he had people waiting for him, and that the Ministry had been trying to get a hold of him all weekend. He said he would be in touch as soon as was convenient, but he wouldn't be in today. She tried to find out where he was. He hung up without answering."

June's stomach muscles knotted together. "That doesn't sound good, does it?"

Alex spoke gravely. "The more he avoids us, the worse it appears. If he doesn't have anything to hide, there's no reason for him not to come forward."

Later that evening, as they lounged on her couch, red wine in hand, jazz on the speakers, she broached the idea of spending a few days at Longworth.

"Absolutely not," Alex said.

She'd expected a discussion. Not this uncompromising attitude. "Excuse me?"

"The last thing I need right now is to be worrying about you, out in the middle of nowhere." His brows lowered in a frown. "Worse than that. You'd be right in the middle of the area where a poaching ring is operating. A poaching ring with at least one member not afraid to commit murder."

She reached out to smooth away the worry lines on his forehead. "I need to get away. I can't stand the suspense, the not knowing. I could barely work today."

"I agree, it might be best if you stayed away from the university for a few days. But you're not going to Longworth Mountain. And certainly not alone." He twisted away from her, putting space between them. "If I had the time I'd go with you, but there's no way I can leave the office now."

June's eyes narrowed. "I'm perfectly capable of looking after myself."

He smacked down his glass, sloshing wine over the rim. "You think Iain couldn't? But he's dead. Dead, June!" He jerked to his feet. "I don't know why, but you're in this up to your neck. You've been attacked twice. I'd feel a lot better if we could get our hands on Fleetham. But we haven't, and I don't think you should be alone. You should move in with me." He hurled the last words at her.

Her heart stuttered. She licked suddenly dry lips. "You want me to move in with you?"

"Just until all this is settled." His mouth was flat and uncompromising. She might have accepted if he had made the offer differently. But not when it was given so grudgingly.

"I am not going into hiding." She stood and faced him across the coffee table, lifting her chin. "I am not going to live my life scared to do what I love, what I need to do for my own sanity. You were threatened, too. Are you going to lock yourself in your house?"

He flung his hands up and spun on his heel to stare out the window. "Of course not."

"Well, I won't either."

Chapter Fourteen

Not much had changed in the three weeks or so since June had last been up Longworth Mountain, despite the fact so much seemed to have changed in the world below. The leaves were fuller on the trees, the bushes more robust, but the air was as sweet and fresh.

When she locked her truck and headed up the mountain, she was afraid she wouldn't experience the sense of peace she normally did. It was a great relief to find the silence held its usual healing power. She paused whenever she wanted, to breathe in the mountain's perfume of rock and pine or listen to the music of songbirds and the chatter of squirrels. Once at the lookout, she performed her usual routines to make sure she wasn't going to be sharing it with any four-legged visitors. When she pulled the makeshift lid off the rain barrel, she discovered a scant amount of brackish water, evidence of the continuing hot, dry weather.

The bright day faded to black night. She embraced the solitude.

Lying on the plywood bed, arms folded behind her head, she smiled ruefully to herself. She'd wanted to get to know Alex better, and she was certainly doing so. His vehement reaction to her plan still shocked her.

Last night, after she had bluntly repeated her intention of going out alone, silence stretched between them. She'd watched his reflection in the window. His eyes were hooded and dark, and she couldn't read his thoughts. After aching minutes, he turned to her.

"Fine. You do what you have to do." The words slashed, sharp and steely. "And so will I." He stomped through the door, snapping it shut behind him.

She'd sent him a text message when she left the house that morning. By the time she lost cell service on her drive out, he had yet to reply. It was difficult to believe he was too busy to send a ten second text. Obviously he hadn't worked off his mad.

A stray thought slipped into her consciousness as she shifted into sleep. He wouldn't have been so angry with her if he didn't feel some affection for her. Would he?

****

She was about to leave the lookout for a day of hiking when she heard the familiar sound of a helicopter approaching. She slung her pack on her shoulders, then raised a hand to shade her eyes against the brilliant sky. Certain it was Alex, her heart pounded faster.

As the aircraft neared, she realized it was larger than the one Alex had first flown to the mountain. This one was sleek and black with tinted windows, and the identification letters were painted a discreet, almost indiscernible, grey. It performed its dragonfly landing, and she distinguished two figures in the cockpit. She swallowed her disappointment. Neither was Alex. The passenger reached up to remove the headset, and she recognized Richard Fleetham's unmistakable cap of unruly curls.

Her breath caught and her mind raced. Did this mean the investigation had cleared him? Or was there a more sinister reason for his appearance?

She could only brazen it out. She had been caught in the open, and it was obvious the men had seen her. There was nowhere to hide, nowhere to run.

They took their time getting out of the craft. Richard appeared to be arguing, making wide, sweeping gestures. The pilot sat stoically still, responding in short bursts. Her pulse ratcheted up yet another level.

Finally they stepped out of the helicopter. At first she couldn't place the pilot, until memory spiked through her. It was the large, older man who had been with Richard at the restaurant.

Richard approached, hands outstretched in his usual welcoming manner. While June was used to his snapping energy, she sensed he was wound tighter than normal. Slight frown lines crumpled his brow, and he sounded slightly breathless when he spoke.

"My dear, how are you?" He grasped her hands in both of his.

"What are you doing here?" she asked. Afraid her sweaty palms would betray her nervousness, she eased her hands out of his clasp.

"There seems to be some excitement going on back in town, and I decided it was best to come see you."

"How did you know I was here?"

He tapped his finger playfully on the end of her nose. "Oh, I have my ways."

Over his shoulder, the pilot reached into the cockpit and pulled out a long, black case. He placed it on the ground then strode toward them.

"You haven't met my partner, have you?" Richard said. "This is Walter Schwarz-Silber." Schwarz-Silber stood behind Richard, a head taller and many pounds heavier. He gave no response, instead pinning June with a glare.

She shuddered, as if something slimy had oozed down the back of her neck. She dragged her attention back to Richard. “What do you mean, partner?”

“My, my, you are full of questions today, aren’t you?” He gave her one of his wide, open grins. “You seem ready for a hike. Why don’t we join you? I’ll get my pack from the helicopter.”

He took her arm above the elbow and led her to the machine. She yearned to dig in her heels and yank out of his grip, but Schwarz-Silber’s bulk was close behind. The muscles between her shoulder blades pulled tight.

“Actually, I was out already this morning,” she lied. “I was on my way in for a rest when you landed. I’ve always preferred hiking early in the day. It seems so much more primitive and wild.” Aware she was babbling, she bit her lip and continued more moderately. “You and Mr. Schwarz-Silber can go on without me, I’m sure. Besides,” she added, inspired, “I have to stick around the tower. I’m expecting Alex today. He said he’d be coming by sometime this morning.”

Richard released her to open the cockpit door and drag out a small pack. She controlled the urge to run. “Oh, I don’t think he’ll be coming out today. He’s going to be busy with other things.” He chuckled, and the sound sent spiders skittering up June’s spine.

“Why, what’s happened?” Fear was a hot knife at her throat. “What’s happened?”

“Nothing. Nothing to concern you,” Richard soothed, insincerity seeping. “We simply made sure he’d be occupied today, so the three of us could have a good visit.” He studied her. “Of course, he’ll have other things to worry about, soon enough. From all I hear, he's quite fond of you."

Her skin crawled at the oily tone in Fleetham's voice and the veiled threat in his eyes. How could she have been so naive, never to have seen through to the egotism and arrogance? She clung to the door frame, damp fingers struggling for a grip. "I'm not going with you."

His eyes slid over her shoulder. "Oh, I think you are."

She swivelled her head. Schwarz-Silber knelt before her, his pose anything but subservient. He had opened the carrying case, and was methodically assembling a large rifle. Her legs threatened to buckle. She forced herself to stay upright. Schwarz-Silber looked at her, his cold blue eyes professionally calm. When he spoke, his voice was deep and gravelly, with a strong, coarse accent, but his English was precise. "You will come with us," he said. "And you will do everything we tell you to." He snapped the case shut and rose to his feet, the rifle held loosely in both hands. "Let's go."

June focused fiercely on where she placed her feet as Fleetham led them over the edge of the mountain. If she engrossed herself in what was directly ahead, maybe she'd be able to ignore what was too close behind. She'd seen the ease with which Schwarz-Silber carried the heavy rifle, one hand at the trigger and one on the barrel. Her head spun, thinking of all that firepower less than a heartbeat away from her undefended back. The sky darkened as light-headedness greyed her vision, but she breathed deeply and it cleared.

Travelling in silence, they dropped down to the valley floor, then moved along the edge of the natural depression. She trod carefully, left foot, right foot. After a few minutes her first fright receded, and she was able to plan further than her next step. This was her mountain, her place. She was going to get away. All she had to do was be ready.

They headed toward the first kill site June and Alex had discovered, with Fleetham continually scanning the sky above and keeping in the shadow of the rock wall to their left. When they reached the narrow crevasse where the grizzly's carcass had been hidden, Fleetham stopped. "We'll rest here for a bit," he said. "I do hope you have water with you, because Walter and I didn't bring enough for you to share."

June released her canteen without taking off her pack. No freaking way was she going to be separated from her supplies, even for a second. If—no, when—she escaped, she might need what was in it. The water was a balm to her dry throat. She drank sparingly.

Schwarz-Silber sat quietly, sipping from his own bottle. She ignored him, afraid if she worried too much about the weapon he carried, she'd never get the courage to flee. Fleetham wandered over to the crack in the rock wall and peered inside. "Not much left of him," he said wonderingly. "And he was a big guy, too."

What a sad epitaph for a proud, perfect animal. Her memory of the pitiful remnants was vivid. Fleetham's dismissive words kindled rage, at his callousness, his disrespect. And how big a step was it, from killing protected animals to snuffing the life out of a human being? She shoved away the thought of Iain's murder.

"Why, Richard?" she asked.

A drop of water clung to the short hairs of his beard. It flashed in the light as he turned to her. "Money, of course," he said. "And lots of it."

June wanted to slap the self-satisfied look off his face. She jammed her hands between her knees to curb the impulse. "But what about RiverForce? What about your beliefs, your goals? What about all those things you said in meetings, the conferences you spoke at?"

"Getting involved with RiverForce was the brilliant idea of a friend of mine. You see, Walter and I were searching for new—business opportunities, shall we say?—which was one of the reasons I took my position at the university. Northern British Columbia was a prime location to expand our enterprise. My friend suggested I join RiverForce, as a smokescreen, you see?"

"I see," June said bitterly. "I see I was too stupid to see through you."

"Don't worry about that. I was very good, very clever. You weren't the only one fooled." Fleetham's pleased expression darkened. "Everyone was, until that conservation officer of yours. He's the one that set all this off. I still don't know why." He waited for her to answer. She gave no reply, not about to mention Sean's chance sighting. "I am afraid he is going regret his involvement, almost as much as I regret yours. It is too bad. I did like you."

His use of the past tense did not escape her.

Less than a kilometre from the first kill site, Fleetham began to ascend the west wall of the valley. He moved, surefooted but slow, up the steep slope. When they reached the top, he paused, panting heavily. In this state, she could outrun him. But Schwarz-Silber appeared at her shoulder, and he betrayed no signs of fatigue. Testing her limits, she walked a few feet away and scanned the view.

Although they had been hiking for more than an hour, they had climbed back up the mountain on the same side as the tower. She spotted the Fraser River glinting and a break in the trees revealed a short stretch of railway tracks far below. It was an immense relief. Had Fleetham led them further east and north, she would have been out of familiar territory. But now, if she escaped soon, all she would have to do is head downhill, and she should be able to reach the road without too much trouble. Even though it wasn't heavily travelled, there was still enough traffic to ensure she would find help.

Fleetham started down. June hesitated, just for a moment. That was all it took to have the muzzle of Schwarz-Silber's rifle jabbing into her back.

She whirled to face him, arms crossed to ward off another strike. Her eyes met his defiantly.

Slowly he raised the gun in his massive arms. His gaze was empty. Soul-less. It made the slight upward curve of his lips all the more unnerving.

"What is it the English say? You are a cat with nine lives? Once I had you, like this, in the crosshairs. And yet you live."

Her arms fell to her sides. "You? It was you who shot at my truck?"

"Not at your truck." Disgust tinted his voice. "At you. I followed you, crept through the woods, found your truck parked by that very odd house. I watched through the window until I saw you readying to leave. I slashed your tire. I knew it would not be long before you had to stop. It was easy to slip around, find a place from which to shoot."

He knew where her parents lived. She wanted to

vomit.

He sighted down the barrel. The muzzle gaped before her. She couldn't look away, horribly fascinated by the blackness staring back at her.

"Walter!" Fleetham's voice tugged June out of her daze. "We talked about this. You are not allowed to shoot her."

She would have been more relieved if she believed Fleetham had a more merciful plan for her. But his tone was playful, as if holding out a treat to a family pet to make sure it behaved.

Seconds passed. Schwarz-Silber held his position. When he lowered the rifle, June's knees wobbled. He gestured with the gun, and she turned to follow Fleetham.

When she decided to make her move, she'd have to be sure there was lots of cover—or that she disabled the German somehow. A boulder to the head might do it, she considered longingly.

They entered the tree line. She stayed alert, ready to dive into the scrub. But a few metres in, Fleetham stopped next to a large, tangled deadfall.

"Here we are," he said jovially, as if they'd entered a cafe and were about to order mocha lattes. "This should do." He turned to June. "All right, give me your pack."

"No." June shook her head and backed away, but Schwarz-Silber blocked her path. "I'm keeping it with me."

Fleetham sighed. "You've cooperated so nicely. Don't stop now. I want your pack and I will have it." With a casualness more stunning than the blow, he stepped forward and backhanded her across the face.

Her head snapped sideways and she careened into Schwarz-Silber. He shoved her and she fell to her knees. Trembling, she raised one hand to her stinging cheek and willed back the tears burning in her eyes. The humiliation was harder to take than the pain, as was the shock of having a man she'd once admired strike her.

Gone was the jovial, charming professor. In his place stood a cold, hard stranger. A murderer.

She rose to her feet, letting her shoulders sag in defeat.

Then she bolted.

She sprinted downhill, zigzagging through the trees, braced for the boom of the big rifle, the hammering pain of a bullet. Her pack jounced up and down, digging into her shoulders and catching on branches. She lurched over roots and rocks. Fleetham and Schwarz-Silber cursed as they crashed through the bush behind her. She raced doggedly on.

Until her boot caught on an exposed root and sent her flying.

Schwarz-Silber was upon her immediately. She fought him wildly, clawing and biting, but he was too big, too strong. He captured both her wrists in one large hand and punched her in the stomach.

Absolute terror is not being able to breathe.

Schwarz-Silber released her. She collapsed to the ground, writhing. Her mouth opened and closed, but no air reached her starving lungs. The spasm passed, leaving her retching and gasping, cheek pressed to the needle-strewn ground.

Fleetham stood wheezing above her. He reached down and picked up a long, thick stick.

"You shouldn't have run," he huffed out. "Really,

you shouldn't have."

The muscles bunching in his shoulders warned her a fraction of a second before he savagely swung the makeshift club. She tried to avoid the blow, but it caught her above the ear.

It was as if she'd been thrown in the deep end of a swimming pool. The world tilted and turned, spinning uncontrollably. There was no up, no down, no here, no now.

Fleetham said, "That should hold her." Then the stars rocketing behind her eyes faded to black.

****

Alex paced back and forth, his long strides covering the short distance from wall to wall easily. "I hate waiting."

"Really. I couldn't tell. You might want to give the carpet a break."

He and Samantha Cross were in his office at the Ministry. While Alex attempted to release his tension in nervous movement, Samantha sat rigidly still. Her anxiety was betrayed only by the edge of sarcasm in her voice.

It had been an enormous relief to learn Richard Fleetham had been in touch with the RCMP, and had scheduled a meeting for later that morning. He promised no more delays, and had appeared willing, even eager, to answer any and all questions. Fleetham had requested Alex to attend the meeting, but the RCMP had uninvited him in no unspecific terms.

Now they were waiting to hear from the team sent to the university.

Alex pulled out his phone and read June's text again. It simply stated she had left for the mountain. He hadn't replied. Now he felt childish for not doing so, but by this time she'd be out of cell range, and it was too late.

When it came to June, he seemed to lose his normal sense of perspective. He really hadn't handled things well last night. She was free to go where she wanted, when she wanted. They had slept together a couple of times. That didn't give either of them any control over the other. Isn't that the way he'd wanted it? When he'd told her she should come live with him, he couldn't believe the words had issued from his own mouth. And been even more shocked to discover he badly wanted her to say yes. When she'd refused, the strength of his disappointment had him reacting in anger.

He baffled himself.

The meeting had been scheduled for ten a.m. He glared impatiently at the wall clock. It was now twenty minutes after the hour. The interview would take much, much longer, but after all the false starts in the last few days he'd hoped for confirmation it had actually begun.

The phone rang. He snatched it up.

Nelson Manning's voice came wearily over the line. "He didn't show."

"Again?" Alex asked uselessly, furious disbelief storming through him.

"He faked us out. He's not here and his secretary has heard nothing from him. We waited this long, thinking he might have forgotten to tell her, but no dice."

"Damn it, Nelson." Alex said. "Damn it! Where is he?"

"I don't know. The cops are getting righteously pissed off. When they do catch up with him it isn't going to go well."

Alex slammed down the phone. "He didn't show."

Samantha nodded, face grim. "I gathered that."

He opened a filing cabinet drawer, smashed it shut, bursting with frustrated energy. "He's got to be involved. I know it in my gut. We've got to find the damn man."

"He's holed up somewhere. A cabin, someplace he hunts from?"

Alex stared at Samantha, ice clutching his bowels. "Oh, God."

She gave him a puzzled glance. "What?"

"June Brandt. My..." he stumbled to a stop. *My what? Lover, girlfriend, partner?* "The woman I met on Longworth Mountain. She's out there now, on her own. And we don't know where Fleetham is."

"Why would he go there? What does June have to do with anything?"

Itchy fingers of worry clawed up the back of his neck. "She's been attacked twice since I've known her. She works at RiverForce with Fleetham. I can't prove it, but there has to be a connection."

"Then why is she out there on her own?"

Because I let her go. Instead of calmly and sensibly asking her to stay where I could look after her, I pushed her away. "I've got to check on her. I've got to see if she's all right."

Samantha stood up, headed for the door. "Let's go."

Chapter Fifteen

The skin on June's skull was so tight every follicle on her head ached. The pain was most intense on the right side, radiating down her neck into her shoulder. When she tried to lift her hands, she couldn't elevate her arms more than a few centimetres.

Confused, she lay still, fighting through the dizziness. She should open her eyes, take stock of her situation. It took too much effort.

She smelled smoke.

Perplexed but not disturbed, she forced her eyelids up. The sky was cracked and broken, splintered by a black web, like a shattered windshield. She squeezed her eyes shut, bracing against the throbbing in her brain, then opened them carefully once again.

This time, the crazy pattern above resolved itself into tangled branches and tree limbs. More bewildered than ever, she tried to sit up, and managed to struggle to her elbows. That was as far as she could get, but at least she was able to make sense of where she was.

She had been buried in a deadfall of trees. Her baggy cargo shorts, with their multitude of pockets, loops and Velcro fastenings, had been used to ensnare her. Branches were actually inside the straps and bands, binding her to the debris. She still had her backpack on her shoulders, but the straps were twisted around her arms and torso. She was wrapped almost as tight as a strait jacket.

The smell of smoke heightened, and she wriggled around, contorting her body, trying to determine where it was coming from. With the tinder dry conditions in the forest, it wouldn't take long for even a smouldering match to grow into a malevolent blaze. Somewhere behind her head she heard crackling, and a gust of wind blew a cloud of ash toward her. She gagged and choked.

Her struggles were getting her nowhere. Taking a deep breath of the polluted air, she shouted. It was a reflex reaction. One part of her brain knew there was no help nearby. But the other part refused to go quietly.

The stifling smoke grew thicker and thicker. The snapping sounds grew louder and louder. Sweat beaded her face. The crown of her head was scorching. She fought frantically to release herself.

She twisted her neck and caught a glimpse of boiling red flames. Her struggles grew more and more desperate until, finally, she managed to free one of her arms. She squirmed out of the straps of her backpack. Now she could sit up, and get a better view of the situation.

The fire was eating its way through the vast amount of fuel provided by the deadfall, creeping ever closer. Its snapping and popping sounds had given way to a full-throated roar, and sparks fell all about, fed by the dried sap. A large ember shot toward her, and she batted it out before it burned into her pack. She attacked the branches around her legs with renewed vigour.

Hacking and yanking with her hands, she forced the branches to give way. By kicking and bucking with her legs, she was at last able to get to her knees. She broke through the web of dry branches above her. Scratched and bleeding from the bark and needles still clinging to the dead limbs, she struggled out of the confines of the trap.

Exhausted, coughing, panting, she crawled away, dragging her pack with her. She reached a large pine and leaned against the trunk, peering through dry, irritated eyes at the deadfall being greedily devoured. She was having trouble focusing. Her eyes rolled loosely in her head, and the burning light seared her brain.

The fire danced higher and higher. Branches of nearby trees burst into flames. Gathering her strength, she battled her way back up the mountain. The smoke was smothering, and the heat followed her, but she could do nothing to stop the inferno. She had to get out of the forest as quickly as possible.

She clambered out of the treeline. Gulping down great breaths of clear, clean air, she flopped on a large rock and clung to it, as a drowning woman might cling to a life preserver, face pressed to the rough surface. The pounding in her head was so severe she had to fight back nausea. Her arms and legs stung from a multitude of scratches and abrasions.

She pushed herself to a sitting position. Taking careful sips from her water bottle, she considered the situation.

The fire hadn't burned through to the edge of the trees yet, but a huge plume of dark grey smoke gave evidence of its ferocity. The smell of burning wood, often a friendly, welcome scent, was now an ominous menace.

She searched through her pack for her cell phone. To her dismay, but not surprise, the "no service" indicator was displayed on the screen. Hope more than expectation had made her check.

The phone's clock told her more than two hours had passed since she'd been forced to leave the lookout with Fleetham and Schwarz-Silber. She guessed she'd been unconscious for at least half an hour. If they headed straight back, the men would reach their helicopter soon.

She had a decision to make. She must get messages to the authorities, to tell them about Fleetham and Schwarz-Silber as well as the forest fire growling below. She could head straight down the mountain, circling around the flashpoint and intersect with the road, or she could follow the trail in the valley back to the tower, then head down.

With the first option, she would have to find her own way through the bush, as there would be no trail to follow. If the fire spread faster than she anticipated, it could catch up with her. And making it to the road was no guarantee she would meet anyone. If she didn't, she would have to hike back to the village and find a phone there.

With the second option, she ran the risk of meeting Fleetham and Schwarz-Silber at the lookout. Also, there would be no chance of finding help before she reached the village. But she would be able to stay clear of the fire and might even make better time with well-defined, familiar paths to follow.

She dithered a while longer, her aching head making it difficult to think clearly. Her physical state made the decision for her. Bushwhacking through unfamiliar territory was dangerous enough when in good health. The way she felt, she would be much better off backtracking.

She savoured one last tiny sip from her water bottle.

It was about half full, which, if she was careful, should do until she returned to the lookout.

Ruthless determination got her back on her feet, over the ridge, and down into the valley. Abused muscles had stiffened as she'd stewed about what to do. She couldn't remember it happening, but she must have banged her knee. It was swollen and sore, causing her to limp. She forced herself to move just under a level of exertion that would exhaust her meagre energy. Every few minutes she rested briefly. In this cautious way she passed the first kill site.

The valley was wide and open, dotted with clumps of shaggy green willows and dark rugged rocks. She concentrated on moving forward. With every pulse beat, her injuries throbbed. Conquering pain became the centre of her existence.

That was probably the reason she didn't see the grizzly.

It had found a large anthill and was busily engaged in pulling it apart and eating the furious insects swarming over its paws. The bear licked them off like ice cream melting on a cone. Both bear and human noticed each other at the same time. Both froze.

She was only a few metres from the animal. She spoke, her voice calm and quiet though her knees quivered. "Hello, there, big fella. No need to worry about me." Most grizzlies avoided humans, and would back away from a confrontation unless they had to defend themselves, their cubs, or a food source. While the anthill might not seem appetizing to June, the young bear had matted fur and prominent shoulder blades. It looked like it needed whatever sustenance it could find. Despite its scrawniness, it still outweighed her by many kilograms.

It stepped toward her.

She said firmly, "You stay away, now, okay? I need to get past you, and then you can go back to eating those lovely bugs." She raised her arms above her head in a vain effort to appear larger.

The bear peered at her with a flat, dark gaze, swinging heavily back and forth on its front feet.

It bounded toward her. She had no chance to evade.

She dropped to the ground, curling tight into a fetal position. Her hands clasped behind her head, protecting her vulnerable neck. A blow, even though muffled by the bulk of her pack, clacked her teeth together. She pulled her bent legs close to her chest, burying her face. Another blow rolled her over, but she remained clamped in position.

The bear's hot breath ruffled her hair, tickled her ear, as it snuffled around her head. She smelled it, an odd combination of old meat and sweet grass. It made huffing noises low in its throat. A leathery nose brushed against the fingers at the back of her neck. June breathed shallowly and tried to control her racing heartbeat. Her muscles cramped with the strain of holding still. Every fibre in her being urged her to jump to her feet and run.

She nearly lost control when she felt tugging on her shoulders and heard a tearing sound. The bear was biting into her pack, ripping it open. It struggled to shred through the tough nylon material, dragging her along with each pull of its powerful jaws, scraping her across the rough, rocky ground.

****

Alex and Samantha were barely in the air when a plume of smoke, stretching straight up before flattening itself against the sky, became visible.

"Forest fire," Samantha said.

"It's on our way to the lookout." Alex monitored the controls automatically, forcing himself to pay attention to the familiar tasks. He couldn't shake the trepidation that had settled over him. "We'll call in the coordinates."

They skirted the billowing charcoal tower and landed gently onto the rocky mountaintop. Samantha jumped out as soon as it was safe and headed to the grey-sided building. Alex hadn't even had a chance to finish securing the aircraft before she returned.

"No one there. But there's a sleeping bag on the bed and food in the cupboards. She's probably gone for a hike."

"I have to make sure." Alex pulled out a long barrelled rifle from the storage compartment. "She could be anywhere, but let's head toward where we found the first grizzly carcass. If we don't see her after half an hour or so we'll come back here."

They crossed over the mountaintop and scrambled down into the valley, moving purposefully. Alex scanned the area. Nothing but emptiness. Every minute they hiked increased his sense of doom.

They drew around a large scree of boulders, and Alex stopped breathing.

Two hundred metres away a young grizzly dragged a crumpled human body. He saw long blond hair and a familiar red windbreaker. For the first time in his life he understood what it meant to have the world fall out from underneath him.

He stood rooted for an instant, then swung the rifle into position and sighted through the scope. He was perfectly prepared to kill the bear to save June's life, but couldn't get a clear shot. Jerking the barrel toward the sky, he pulled the trigger.

The shot boomed out in the still mountain air.

Aiming once more through the scope, he saw the grizzly raise its muzzle from June's body, but it didn't run.

Again he pointed the gun into the sky. Again the shot crashed like thunder.

****

In one of the bear's attempts to tear open her pack, it had torn June's hand. Blood dripped down her neck. All the terror, all the confusion of the last few hours coalesced into a nightmare she no longer believed she would escape. So when the first shot shattered the air, she didn't realize what it was. But when the next echoed through the valley, it broke through her muddled thoughts.

The pressure on her shoulders disappeared. She lay on her side in the tight little ball that had become her world, eyes firmly closed, tasting the grittiness of dust in her mouth. She heard shouting, but an eerie calm fogged her senses. It wasn't until Alex cradled her in his arms that she recognized his voice.

Slowly she opened her eyes. He hovered over her, face pale under his tan, brown eyes wide. She could tell he was speaking to her, but a buzzing filled her ears and she couldn't hear the words. His face seemed to melt like old film held too long before the projector lamp and everything grew unnaturally bright, before fading to blackness.

She woke to fingers skimming through her hair and Alex's hoarse voice muttering. "It's okay now, it's okay.

I've got you."

Her eyelids flittered, and she struggled to sit up.

"Shhh, shhh," he comforted. "It's okay now, lay back now."

"The bear..." she whispered rustily.

"It's gone, don't worry. The shots chased it away."

Recollection returned in a rush, and she grabbed his wrist. "Alex, Richard was here. He is involved, in everything. He and another man, the one we saw at the restaurant, they started a fire. The fire..." This time he allowed her to get to a sitting position. He supported her with an arm around her shoulders and his bent knee at her back.

"Don't worry. We've already called it in. Sam and I saw it when we flew over. Take a minute, then you can tell me everything." Over his shoulder Samantha Cross, whom she recognized from the airport the dreadful day of Iain's murder, stood four-square and forbidding, scanning the area with a rifle cradled in the crook of her arm. June coughed and Alex handed over his canteen.

She reached out to take it, wincing as the movement fired up scrapes and stings. Pouring water into her mouth, she let it ease her parched tongue, then gulped it down.

Samantha crouched next to them. "What the hell happened to you?" she demanded.

Twinges and spasms coursed through her arms and legs. Her shoulders pounded from the savage wrenching, her swollen knee ached. She told them everything that had occurred since Fleetham and Schwarz-Silber landed on the mountain. Alex's face grew flinty.

"The bear was simply plain bad luck." She leaned, exhausted, against Alex, head resting on his shoulder.

"I'm so glad you came when you did. I didn't know if I was going to get away." Her voice hitched and her throat tightened with tears. She breathed deeply, in through her nose and out through her mouth, and the panic subsided. Alex's arms around her were home and safety.

Hydrating had helped with the light-headedness, and soon she was well enough to stand, but was thankful for Alex's firm grip on her hand as they walked along.

"Why are you here?" she asked as they began the ascent to the lookout. "You couldn't have known I'd be in trouble."

"Fleetham baited us with an appointment this morning. But he didn't show, again. I couldn't shake the feeling he had used the meeting as a distraction. And knowing you were out here, on your own..." She glanced up at an odd note in his voice, but he continued to stare straight ahead. "I had to check. Samantha insisted on coming with me."

To June's extreme relief, they crested the slope and reached the plateau. Instead of the sleek black craft she'd last seen there, the familiar rounded shape of Alex's helicopter rested next to the lookout. By now, sheer stubbornness was all that kept her on her feet, and when he led her to the cabin she folded thankfully into the spindly wooden chair.

He dug through her kit, found a bottle of pain relievers, and handed it to her. She shook a couple into her palm and swallowed them dry, hoping they would take the edge off the misery in her head. As he rolled up her sleeping bag and efficiently packed the rest of her belongings, she fingered the huge tears in her backpack. Lingering traces of futility and fear rippled through her system.

Alex turned to her, worry still haunting his face. He touched her cheek in a caress so light she barely felt it. “Ready to go?”

She nodded. Samantha waited by the trailhead leading down to Longworth village. June handed over her keys. It had been decided Samantha would hike down and drive June’s truck back into Prince George while Alex and June returned in the helicopter. They waited until Samantha disappeared into the trees, then lifted off and set their course for home.

Chapter Sixteen

June resisted Alex's attempts to take her to the hospital once they arrived in the city.

"All I want right now is a shower," she insisted.

"You've probably got a concussion," accused Alex, "so you're in no shape to decide what you need. I'm bringing you in."

"I want a shower, and I want it now." She hugged her arms across her body. "My head hurts, along with a few more bits of me, but I can handle it. I need to get cleaned up and have a rest, in my own house."

He manoeuvred his Jeep out of the airport parking lot. "We have to let the RCMP know what's going on."

"You can call them from my place. Please, Alex. I want to go home. With you."

The stern frown on his face softened. "Okay," he said, "but I'm keeping an eye on you. If you don't feel better soon, you're going to the hospital if I have to hogtie you."

"Deal." She closed her eyes and allowed herself to relax, trusting his word. She must have dozed off, because the next thing she knew, Alex was opening her door and scooping her up in his arms.

"Put me down," she said, words slurred with fatigue. "I'm perfectly capable of walking." He ignored her and continued to the front door.

"I'll get your stuff from the Jeep." He lowered her

to her feet so she could use her key. "You get in the shower."

It was pure delight to strip out of her filthy, sweaty T-shirt and shorts, peel off the grimy socks and stand naked under the steaming spray. Water streamed through her hair, washing the blood and dirt down the drain. She lathered thoroughly, careful with the goose egg over her ear, then soaped the rest of her body, flinching as various scrapes, dulled during the trip home, woke to stinging, burning life.

She wrapped herself in her robe and headed back to the living room. Alex sat on the couch, a pad of paper on the coffee table in front of him, making notes and grunting into the phone. He watched her approach, a tiny smile lighting his eyes.

"Okay, got it," he said. He held out a hand, and when she took it, gently urged her down onto the couch next to him. His thumb massaged her knuckles as he continued his conversation. "Yes. We'll be here. You can get me on my cell." He disconnected and tossed his phone on the table. "You seem better." He twisted a damp strand of hair between his fingers.

"I feel better." It wasn't a total lie.

"You need to eat."

Faintly nauseous from the headache, the thought of food made her shudder. "I'm not hungry. Who were you talking to?"

"I'm going to make you some soup. You must have a can I can open."

"My hero," June teased, but her heart stuttered when she realized she'd spoken the truth. "Who were you speaking to?" she repeated.

"The RCMP. But you don't have to worry about

that for now. I told them everything, including the description of the helicopter. You still can't remember the call letters, can you?"

She shook her head. "I'm sorry I didn't notice. I was too stunned after I realized it was Richard inside."

"They'll make enquiries at the airports around here. Chances are someone will know about it. The cops will want to talk to you themselves, but I've put them off until tomorrow. Now, where's that soup? And shouldn't we call your parents?"

"Not now. Not yet. After all, I'm fine, and there's nothing they can do. I want to be here, in my safe little house, the two of us." Alex seemed to want to argue the point, but he let it ride and went to the kitchen to dig up something to eat.

She let him fuss around her, partly because he insisted, partly because she couldn't deny how weak she felt. At first she was amused by all the attention. Then it started to make her itchy.

"Alex, stop hovering." She patted the couch. "Come sit with me."

He smoothed a hand down her arm as he sat beside her. "You're sure you don't need anything?"

She chuckled, even though it sent small stabs of pain through her skull. "I need you to stop asking me if I need anything. Can we just sit and be quiet, together, for a while?"

"You can sleep if you want. I'll have to wake you every hour or so, because of your concussion." He placed a pillow on his thighs and patted it.

"I don't have a concussion. And I don't want to sleep." But she curled her feet up and laid her head on the pillow. "I want to be here, with you, and enjoy being alive."

****

It had taken a lot of willpower for Alex to let June leave his sight. He'd listened outside the bathroom door, only moving to the living room to make his phone calls after the water had turned off.

She lay beside him now, pale and vulnerable, but he consoled himself with the press of her shoulder against his thigh and by watching the pulse beat in her neck. He sat still and quiet, hoping she would succumb to sleep despite her intentions.

Tenderly he feathered his hand over the bright hair and brushed the large bump above her ear. A muscle jumped in his temple. He couldn't stop his hand from shaking as he stroked her cheek with the back of his fingers.

She lifted her face toward him and raised an eyebrow. "What?"

He worked some saliva into his dry mouth. "I thought I was scared when you called after you'd been shot at. I thought that was fear. But it was nothing—nothing!—compared to what I felt today, when I came down the path, saw that grizzly mauling you." The memory was so raw, so fresh, it still tore at him. "It kept dragging you along. You weren't moving. I couldn't tell if you were alive or dead." He never wanted to feel that way again, unable to draw a full breath, his heart expanding, everything stretching tight.

She rolled over and snuggled closer. "When I heard that rifle boom, I didn't even care if it was Schwarz-Silber coming back, if he got that bear off me."

"I should have shot it. I would have, but I was afraid of hitting you. And then when it ran, all I could think of was getting to you as fast as possible. I prayed you were alive." He, who had rarely if ever prayed before. She reached to touch his face, and he grasped her hand, holding it tightly, kissing her knuckles. His control broke, and he crushed her to his chest, burying his face in her hair. "God, oh God. I thought I'd lost you. I thought you were dead."

He rocked with her until the ferociousness of his emotions eased and his breathing slowed.

With a hand on the back of his neck, she drew him down to her. Her lips firm against his, the kiss was a balm to his tattered soul, and he sank into her, changing the angle, deepening it.

The rage and fear he had bottled up became molten, melting into need. He wanted to be tender, to be careful of her wounds, but desperation filled him, made him reckless. His mouth devoured the delicate skin of her neck, scented with lemon from her shower, and his hands wrapped around her torso, lifting her to mould her once again to his body.

He slipped his arms under her knees. Cradling her against him, he stood up. "I need you, now. I need to know you're all right, that you're mine, that you'll always be mine." She shivered and he hesitated, knowing he was asking too much of her.

Her arms linked tightly around his neck, her mouth grazed moistly down his throat. "Last door on the right," she murmured.

He laid her on the bed, unbelted her robe, and spread it open. Her body was leanly muscled, her breasts small, hips a subtle sweep. His finger circled the dark mole next to her belly-button.

She gazed at him with languorous eyes. He

unbuttoned his shirt, unbuckled his trousers. When he was naked she sat up and wriggled out of her robe, letting it slip silkily off her shoulders, then reached for him.

Air hissed through his teeth as her cool fingers wrapped around his hard, hot length. His hands dove into her damp, tousled hair, holding on, encouraging her to explore his body. Her breath danced across his stomach. He groaned, the thin threads of control slipping, silvery strands stretched to breaking point. When her fingers touched the tip of his shaft, he recoiled and captured her wrist.

"Doesn't that feel good?" she said, her voice hesitant.

"Dear lord," he ground out. "Too good."

Anxiety transformed to mischievousness. "I like it, too." She rubbed him again, and he growled deep in his throat.

His legs were on the verge of collapse. If she kept touching him he was going to lose all sense of restraint. He reached down with both hands to cup her breasts, then eased himself from her hold and knelt in front of her. Toying with one nipple with his fingers, he tantalized the other with his tongue and was rewarded with whimpers of pleasure.

She seemed to liquify under his hands, his mouth, and flowed backward until she was lying on the bed. He followed her, licking, sucking. Sensations blended together in a heady swirl of lust and love. He slid into her wet and ready warmth. Only then did he allow himself to let go, to bury himself in her over and over again. She wrapped her legs around him and surrounded him, enfolded him. Arching passionately against him, she tightened. He thrust one last time.

They lay together, trembling, panting with exertion. He reveled in the long length of her pressed against him, the softness of her breasts brushing his chest as they breathed, the strong muscles of her thighs, the slenderness of her waist.

"Can you hear my heart?" she whispered. "I think it's beating out of my chest."

It came to him then, and the knowledge was so right, so perfect, it brought a tranquility he had never known. "I love you." He marveled at how easy it was to say. His fingers cupped her breast absently, his eyes locked on hers.

She lay motionless, searching his face. He waited. She remained silent. His sensation of peace dimmed. "Did you hear me? I love you, June."

"You love me?" she asked.

"I think I've been denying it to myself for days. But today, when I found you on the mountain...I couldn't pretend anymore." His hands cradled her face. For the second time that day he prayed. *Please, God. Please let her love me back.*

Deep in her eyes a light glimmered. This time when she spoke he heard the joy, the anticipation. "You love me?"

"I do." One corner of his mouth quirked self-consciously. "I never believed I'd say that to anyone. But then I met you, and I've never known anyone like you before. I don't think I could live without you. The idea of not having you in my life makes me crazy."

"You're not having a reaction to all the excitement, are you?"

This time he gave her a full on grin. "I'm positive.

Want me to say it again?" She nodded. "I love you."

She lifted her hand, cupping the hard edge of his jaw. "Damn right you do. And guess what? I love you, too."

Elation burst inside him. He drank in the exultant gleam in her eyes, rejoiced in the gleeful curve of her lips, a mirror to his own. He wrapped his arms around her and dragged her on top of him, hugging her fiercely. "Say it again," he said, hoarse with emotion. "Tell me again."

A carefree giggle bubbled out of her throat. "I love you." She kissed his cheek. "I love you." And his other cheek. "I love you." And when her lips met his, he found home.

****

June's first view when she opened her eyes the next morning was Alex, lying on his back on top of the bed covers, arms crossed over his chest. Stubble shadowed his strong jaw, and despite sleeping soundly at the moment, dark bruises under his eyes attested to a disturbed night. She had vague memories of him throughout the wee hours, waking her to ask simple questions, watching for the dangerous symptoms of concussion, each time allowing her to slip back into a healing sleep.

Scrapes and bruises tugged at her, and her knee was slightly swollen, but the headache had almost disappeared. Carefully she slipped out of the sheets and sat on the edge of the bed, waiting for any sign of light-headedness or nausea. When all seemed well, she limped out of the room, shrugging into her robe on her way to the kitchen.

The display on the coffee machine told her it was

barely nine o'clock. While the liquid dripped into the pot, dispersing delicious curls of caffeine-laden scent into the air, she puttered around the room, putting away the dishes Alex had washed the night before.

She filled two mugs and headed back to the bedroom. He lay as she had left him. She sat on the edge of the bed, and he still did not stir. The knowledge that he loved her was so big, so new, she could hardly believe it. She stroked her mouth against his. His eyes opened, dark and drowsy.

"How are you feeling?" His voice was gruff. He cleared his throat, then gave her a hopeful look. "Is that coffee?" He shifted to rest against the headboard and gratefully took the mug she handed him.

She hugged her own cup with both hands, enjoying the heat seeping through the porcelain. "I feel almost one hundred percent, thanks to you."

"Anytime." He studied her over the lip of his mug. "How's the headache?"

"Hanging on, but not bad. Much better, in fact." Unaccountably, she felt shy, wondering how to bring up the subject she most wanted to talk about.

"I didn't dream last night, did I?"

She narrowed her eyes at him. "Dream what?"

"That you told me you loved me?"

Relief surged through her. She smacked his knee. "I've wanted to tell you for days. I was waiting for you to see the light. Too bad it took a near death experience—mine—before you did."

The glow in his eyes set up a throbbing in her veins. "I love you, June. And I've never been happier about anything in my life."

They sat, smiling idiotically at each other. She blew

on her coffee, took a sip. "So, what happens now?"

He sputtered into his mug. "What, about us? Can't a guy have a few months to get used to the idea?"

She stared blankly at him, then the penny dropped. Her snicker rolled into a howl of mirth. She laughed until her sides ached, until tears rolled down her cheeks. He was forced to rescue her tilting coffee cup.

"Today," she hiccoughed. "I meant what happens today. Oh, God. You should have seen your face."

He gave her hair a quick yank. "All right, that's enough out of you. If that's the case, what happens now is that you have breakfast, and get more rest."

She wiped the last of her tears on the bed sheet. "What about Richard and Schwarz-Silber? Did you hear anything last night after I fell asleep?"

"Samantha brought back your truck. The keys are in the kitchen."

"Good. What else?" His expression betrayed his urge to dodge her questions, to hide knowledge from her. "Tell me, Alex."

"Detective George called," he said reluctantly.

"Who's that?"

"The younger of the two investigators into Iain Prevost's murder. You met him at my office the day you brought the note."

She curled her legs under her and sat cross-legged on the bed. Her knee complained but the stretch felt good. "What did he say?"

"They haven't found any sign of the helicopter, Fleetham or Schwarz-Silber." His eyes drifted down and she realized her robe gaped open slightly. She covered herself and he took a gulp of hot coffee, wincing.

She huffed out a breath. "So now what? What do

we do?"

"Detective George wants us to go into the detachment today so you can give your report directly. Then we come home. And we wait."

"Wait!" There must be something they could do, she thought in disgust.

He clasped her hand. "We wait. The RCMP has it under control. We could do more harm than good if we go off on our own. You have to trust them to do their job."

She firmed her lips. "Fine. I'll get dressed and we'll go in." She put her coffee down with a thump and stomped off down the hall.

Chapter Seventeen

Alex and June were leaving the RCMP detachment when her cell phone rang. Tabitha Scala's voice bounced enthusiastically out of the speaker.

"June, I wasn't sure I'd get a hold of you. I thought you were going camping."

"I did go out of town for a couple of days, but my trip was...cut short."

"Isn't that totally lucky. For me, I mean." Tabitha's laughter trilled. "I'm having a bit of a soiree tonight, and I'd love it if you could come."

Alex lifted an enquiring eyebrow, and she motioned for him to continue out of the parking lot. Their next stop was her parents' home. June hadn't wanted to worry them since everything had turned out fine, but Alex had insisted. Even though she hadn't mentioned Fleetham and Schwarz-Silber at all, because she wasn't sure what the RCMP would like kept confidential, and had glossed over the grizzly attack, Monica and Karl had insisted she come out so they could see for themselves she was okay.

"Tabitha, I'm sorry. But I don't think I'm up to it. I came back into town early because I wasn't...wasn't feeling well." She ignored a quiet snort from the driver's seat. "I really need an early night."

"Don't say that. It's a party in honour of Richard. He's been nominated for an award..."

She let Tabitha continue, but covered up the mouthpiece and said, “Tabitha Scala. I think I’ve mentioned her before. One of Richard’s groupies.” He nodded. “She says she’s having a party tonight because Richard’s getting an award.”

Alex’s eyebrows drew together. “And he’s going to be there?”

June couldn’t imagine him waltzing casually into a party, but she broke into Tabitha’s excited chatter to ask.

“You’d think so, wouldn’t you, but he says he probably won’t be able to make it.” The other woman’s disappointment was evident.

“When did you talk to him? Did he say where he was?”

“I spoke to him day before yesterday. He said he might have to go out of town, but that I should have the party anyway, because the award is really a celebration of everyone in RiverForce. You have to come, June.”

“I don’t know.”

“Please say you will. Everyone else will be there, they promised me.”

The wistfulness in the other woman’s voice had June weakening. “Well...”

“Oh,” squealed Tabitha, “You will! Seven o’clock tonight, my place. And bring a friend if you want. I know, bring your game warden fellow.”

“Conservation officer, and I’ll see. He might not be available.” She tapped off her phone.

They left the busy downtown streets and headed out on the highway. “Does she really think Fleetham’s going to be there?” Alex asked.

June filled him in on the whole conversation. “I have such trouble telling her no. She’s like a leftover from the sixties, and she talks like a twelve-year-old girl half the time, but I like her. I figure I'll go for an hour or so, then plead a headache." Traces of pain flickered occasionally inside her head, and she was sure by later tonight she wouldn't be telling a complete lie.

"I'm coming with you. It sounded like I was invited." He took the turn into the Brandt's driveway.

"You are, but honestly, you don't have to."

"I'm coming, June." He parked next to the garage. "Until Fleetham and Schwarz-Silber are found, I'm not leaving you alone." Determination jutted in the set of his jaw and resolve gleamed in his eye.

She skimmed the tips of her fingers over his knuckles as he gripped the steering wheel. "Somehow, I knew you'd say that. Thank you. Now, let's go show Mom and Dad I still have all my limbs."

****

"You really didn't have to come."

The early evening shimmered with light as they headed north. Tabitha lived a half hour or so out of town, in a rural area of small farms and large residential lots dotted with all manner of homes, from custom built dwellings to double wide trailers.

"I know."

"If you had stayed home I'd have an excuse other than a headache to get away. I could say I had to meet you."

Alex glared at her, exasperated. "Do you have a headache now? Because I'm beginning to get one."

June frowned. "I'm still planning on faking one about an hour after we arrive. I wish I hadn't agreed to come. Turn right at Salmon Valley."

They crossed a blue metal bridge and exited the

main highway, merging onto a narrow two lane road. It curved and cornered, following the twists of the modest river flowing next to it. A few minutes later she steered him to the driveway of a small house with staid white siding offset by vibrant purple shutters and trim. Tabitha's ancient VW bug was parked next to a barn with a weathered shingle roof and grey walls. The pebbly river sparkled beyond a screen of towering cottonwoods.

"You've been here before?"

They stepped out of the Jeep, June carrying a bottle of wine she'd brought as a hostess gift. "Tabitha had a barbeque a year or so ago for the RiverForce crew. It wasn't long after Richard arrived at the university, actually. We had a great time." Alex opened the low gate in the white board fence separating the drive from the front garden, and they walked up the slate path. "I don't imagine she'll have another this year," she added gloomily.

Alex knocked on the door, also vividly plum. It opened immediately.

Tabitha wore jeans instead of her normal caftan and leggings. A fuchsia tunic, clashing with both the door and her own red hair, draped her to mid-thigh. It was belted around her thin waist with twisted strands of bright yellow cord.

"June! And your game warden! Come in, come in!" She ushered them into a tiny entryway and closed the door behind them.

It bothered June that Tabitha couldn't get Alex's designation right. "It's conservation officer, not game warden. They haven't been called game wardens for fifty years." She held out the bottle of wine. "I brought this for you."

"How sweet! Hold on to it and come through with me. We'll put it in the kitchen. You're the first to arrive."

June stumbled to a halt when Alex stopped short in front of her. Peering past him, she remembered her own stunned reaction to Tabitha's fascinating home.

The miniscule hall led into a completely open floor plan where living room, dining area, and kitchen all flowed together. Fading amber sunlight beamed through wide windows, making them appear paned in golden glass. But what really rocketed to attention were the walls those windows were set in.

Each was a different deep hue—magenta, turquoise, daffodil yellow and a violet so dark as to be almost black. On that dynamic background, in every space available, hung a multitude of miscellaneous artwork, from masks and weavings to framed oils and movie posters, adding their own varied rainbows. At first glance it appeared that area rugs were scattered over the battered yet neutral grey oak floor, but these "rugs," were actually kaleidoscopic murals painted on the wood. Furniture, in an odd collection of styles, from ornately carved antiques to futuristic chrome and glass, filled the space.

The buoyant energy of the room did little to dispel the unease fluttering along June's nerves. She nudged Alex out of his speechless contemplation, and they followed Tabitha to the back of the house. "Who else did you say is coming?" she asked.

"Oh, all sorts of people are on their way, even though it was rather late notice. Can I just say again how delighted I am that you both could make it?"

Finally June was able to pin down at least one of the things tickling her subconscious. There were no party preparations at all—no bowls of chips, vegetable platters, trays of drinks—and nothing to indicate they had interrupted those preparations.

She frowned. "Tabitha..." she started, only to have the question she was about to ask dry to dust in her mouth. A door, barely visible as it was painted the same colour as its wall, opened, and Richard Fleetham and Walter Schwarz-Silber emerged.

Stunned by their sudden appearance, June blurted out, "What are you doing here? The cops, the CO's, everyone's looking for you."

Alex, standing to her right admiring the view out the window, spun on his heel. He advanced swiftly to her side.

She didn't take her eyes off the other men. Fleetham's public relations veneer of friendly superiority was evident, but Schwarz-Silber's cold, flat demeanour had been replaced by an aura of sheer disbelief, underscored with rage.

"And it is you, you who have made this happen." His clipped accent was more noticeable than ever, magnified by fury. "You were not supposed to get off the mountain. I told Richard I should shoot you, but he was soft, wanted to make it seem an accident."

"Now, now," soothed Fleetham. "We've discussed that, Walter, and I've come to realize your way may have been the better option. But all is not lost. We still have time to correct the mistake."

"Yah, we will correct this mistake." Schwarz-Silber reached into the room in which the men had been waiting and pulled out a rifle. It was nastily familiar to

June. “Since you have been involved, everything has gone wrong.” Frustration spewed from him like a cloud, hatred in his eyes. Alex thrust forward, shielding June with his body. Schwarz-Silber raised the rifle and motioned with the barrel. “Stay back. Do not come nearer.”

Alex held his ground. His cool gaze switched to Tabitha. “You’re in on this, too, aren’t you?”

She shrugged and crossed the floor to stand next to Fleetham. They made an arresting couple, both of a height, her flaming red hair a brilliant foil for the curling, springy blackness of his. She stroked his chest languidly, and his arm encircled her waist. “What’s a woman to do? She’s got to take care of her own best interests, doesn’t she?”

The little girl scattiness had vanished from her voice, and from the way Fleetham beamed at her, it was obvious she was not a simple sidekick, but a full partner in the enterprise.

June’s world tilted. She struggled to keep her equilibrium. Her fingers squeezed the neck of the wine bottle she still held. “You’re a part of this, too? The poaching? Murder?”

Tabitha made a small moue of distaste and scowled viciously at Schwarz-Silber. “That was definitely a mistake. Richard said *he* was working,” she gestured with her chin to Alex, “so we thought he would be sent out. Walter was supposed to use his fists to encourage him to lay off the investigation. But instead, he used neither his brain nor his fists.” Her tone was scathing. “And there we were, stuck in the middle of a murder investigation.”

“You selfish, cold-hearted bitch.” Contempt dripped

from each quiet word. "And you..." his scorn switched to Fleetham. "Hiding behind an organization whose sole purpose is to stop people like you. I despise you."

Tabitha took two strides forward. She slapped Alex across the cheek, the crack echoing through the stunned silence. "You will not speak to him that way," she hissed.

The blow twisted Alex toward June. His profile was frozen, hard and unforgiving. Instinctively she reached for him, but he straightened immediately and raised one hand slowly to his jaw.

"I'll speak to him any damn way I want." He gritted the words out through tight lips. Taut muscles betrayed his longing to take action. Past his rigid shoulder the barrel of the rifle held its deadly aim. June gripped his upper arm, silently willing him to be careful.

"Tchahh!" Schwarz-Silber made a harsh, guttural sound of derision. "You say I do not use my brains. This is not smart, this arguing. It is time to finish this. Already too many chances this one has been given."

June's first stunned astonishment had faded. "Chances? What chances?" Her brain whirled, dreaming up and discarding various plans. She needed more time.

"Nothing," Fleetham said sullenly, as Tabitha bit out, "Shut up, Walter."

The puzzle pieces clicked. Her eyes dropped to the heavy, black army boots Schwarz-Silber wore. "You were the motorcycle rider?"

He bared his teeth. "Many times since that night I have wished to have hit you harder."

She worked up a sneer. "No wonder you called me a cat with nine lives. You don't seem to have much luck killing me, do you?" Alex tried to tug his arm out of her grasp, but she held on. "Even when you had me clear in your sights, when you shot at me on my way home from my parents."

"Shot at you?" Tabitha scoffed. "He never shot at you. Or you would be dead." Then she noticed the disgruntled expression on the German's face. "What is she talking about? What the hell did you do?"

Schwarz-Silber turned to Tabitha, eyes glittering, mouth opening to deliver a retort. The muzzle of the gun drooped fractionally. Alex sprang forward. Batting the weapon away with one hand, he drove his fist into the bigger man's belly. Air whooshed out of Schwarz-Silber's lungs. Alex snagged the barrel. Schwarz-Silber reversed his grip and brought the stock up viciously, slashing against Alex's temple. He crumpled to the floor.

With a primitive yell, June jumped forward. She smashed the heavy glass wine bottle on Schwarz-Silber's head. He crashed to the wooden boards, the gun spinning free. She dove for it. Her fingers grazed the cool, burnished metal. A bare foot stomped on her hand, grinding the bones together with crushing force, and she cried out.

Fleetham snatched up the rifle. Her mission thwarted, June dragged her hand out from under Tabitha's heel and crawled to Alex. He crouched on one knee, a hand pressed to his face, blood seeping through his fingers.

"Let me see." June sucked in her breath at the nasty scrape. She looked up at Tabitha. "I need a wet cloth. I need something to hold against it, to clean it."

"Oh, for crying out loud." Tabitha reached down and jerked June up. "Walter's right. Let's get this over with. Richard, make sure that one doesn't move. You, put your hands together." She unwound her belt, and June realized it didn't only look like rope, it actually was. Tabitha tied her wrists tightly together, then, using another strand from around her waist, did the same to Alex, still kneeling on the floor. He said nothing, but glowered with unnerving intensity at Fleetham.

Tabitha booted Schwarz-Silber none too gently in the ribs as he lay groaning on the floor. "Get up. You'll drive your SUV. We'll go with these two, like we planned."

Schwarz-Silber staggered to his feet, holding his head, eyes glassy. They headed to the door, June and Alex in front, the others shepherding them from behind.

Tabitha's house was secluded enough that Fleetham was able to keep the rifle trained at June and Alex as they walked to the Jeep.

"Alex in the passenger seat, June in the back with Richard." Tabitha directed. "I'll drive." She gave Alex a push when he didn't move fast enough. "Richard will have the rifle on June the entire time. You will behave."

June climbed clumsily into the narrow back seat behind the driver. She struggled into position. Fleetham pulled the shoulder strap across her body, slipping the clasp between her linked arms. With the belt locked, her hands were trapped, one over and one under the webbed material.

Schwarz-Silber dragged open the doors of the small barn and disappeared inside. He drove out in a silver SUV. Leading the small convoy down the driveway and out onto the main highway, he turned north. Tabitha appeared calm, but she rode hard on his bumper, and was constantly having to back off.

June's hand throbbed. Her wrists burned from the harsh nylon rope wrapped tightly around them. The taste of fear was strong in her mouth. She cherished every sensation. They meant she was alive.

She sat upright, alert to any chance she might have to turn the tables. In front of her, Alex's body slanted away from Tabitha. Muscles flexed subtly in his neck and shoulders, and June realized he was trying to work his hands free. She hadn't seen how Tabitha had fastened his seat belt. Maybe she hadn't been as devious as Fleetham.

Here, at least, was something she could do. She could keep them distracted.

She turned to Fleetham. The cramped interior forced him to hold the long gun pointing upward, the muzzle under her chin. But with both her and Alex restrained, he'd relaxed enough to let his finger fall off the trigger. He noticed her watching him and gave a faintly apologetic shrug.

"All this, it's for the money?" she asked, letting her disgust tinge the words.

Her repugnance didn't seem to annoy Fleetham. He reminded her of a small boy caught in a minor misdemeanour. "I'm afraid so, my dear. It probably seems sordid to you, but once you've tasted big money, it's so hard to go back to a professor's salary."

"Why did you hire me to work at RiverForce?"

She was amazed to see a sheepish grin cross his face. "I thought it might keep you occupied, so you'd stay away from the investigation." He regarded her solemnly. "I am truly sorry you are mixed up in this. I did warn you away."

They accelerated up the large hill leading out of the

river valley and continued north. "This whole enterprise has been a disaster, ever since the two of you met up on Longworth Mountain," Tabitha said. She eased off the gas after creeping too close to Schwarz-Silber yet again. "Walter told me how he fired warning shots that day, and what do the two of you do? Try to find the shooter. What reasonable human being goes toward the sound of gunfire? You forced him to hide. He was not happy."

The right hand indicator blinked on the vehicle in front, and Tabitha followed suit.

"Who put the note on my windshield?"

Tabitha answered, a small, cruel smile on her lips. "That was me. I was so pissed that Walter had killed the wrong man, I'm afraid I needed to vent."

Schwarz-Silber turned onto a narrow gravel road. It travelled straight through a cleared area for a hundred metres or so, before disappearing into a forest of thick, straight pine. Dust kicked up behind, hanging in the still evening air.

"You shouldn't let that bother you, darling," Fleetham said. "It did no damage in the end." He leaned forward to pat his lover's arm. Alex shifted in his seat, glancing over his shoulder. His gaze sharpened. The rifle had dropped onto Fleetham's thigh, the long barrel now laying across June's knee. He lifted his eyes to hers. She dipped her chin in a tiny nod.

Alex braced his back against the door. The Jeep swung onto the side road, and at the apex of its turn, he jackknifed his body, kicking out brutally. One foot struck Tabitha in the shoulder. The other crushed her fingers against the steering wheel. Without releasing the pressure on the hand on the wheel, Alex kicked upward with his left leg. June flinched at the snap of breaking bone. Tabitha screamed.

Alex's sudden moves shocked Fleetham into immobility. June grappled for the rifle, dragging it out of his slack hold in a two handed grip made necessary by her bonds. Fleetham made a belated grab for the gun. Hampered by her seat belt, June turned her shoulders and attempted to block him. Her palms were slick with sweat. Inch by inch, the muzzle slipped through her fingers.

The Jeep swerved viciously. The motion threw Fleetham into June. They both lost their holds on the rifle and it fell to the floor. Fleetham bent forward to retrieve it. She seized handfuls of his abundant curls and yanked. Fleetham shouted and tried to pry her fingers out of his hair. She clutched tighter.

Tabitha shrieked repeatedly, cradling her broken arm. It was impossible for Alex to reach the uncontrolled steering wheel. The Jeep flew forward, diving into the deep ditch. Tabitha's head bashed against the steering column. Fleetham was propelled between the front bucket seats.

In the sudden stillness June panted, dazedly staring at the fistfuls of dark hair in her hands.

Chapter Eighteen

Fleetham sprawled on his side, draped awkwardly against Alex. Shoving him out of the way, Alex struggled to undo his seat belt, twisting his wrists painfully, cramping his fingers. He finally managed it and shot out of the Jeep.

"June! Are you all right?" He clambered around the back of the vehicle, now slanting to the sky, and wrenched open the door. "Can you walk? Are you okay?" He released her seat belt. She sagged against him and he helped her out. "I had to take the chance. I couldn't think of anything else to do." His hands, still bound together, shook as they stroked her face, her shoulder.

She drew in a deep breath and let it out deliberately. "I'm fine." Her eyes were hazed with shock, but he couldn't see any injuries. "I think. Better than them, anyway." She squinted into the Jeep. Tabitha sprawled over the steering wheel, eyes closed, blood trickling from her nose. Her chest rose and fell rhythmically. Fleetham made a feeble attempt to extricate himself, but collapsed with a groan. "What about Schwarz-Silber?"

Alex reached in and managed to lift out the rifle. Together they scrambled onto the road. The silver SUV had stopped up ahead. Schwarz-Silber stood, one foot on the road and one in the vehicle, looking over his shoulder toward the wreck.

On the highway, a baby blue pickup, jacked up high on huge tires, screeched to a halt. The driver leaped down. The appearance of a witness decided Schwarz-Silber. He slammed the door shut and sped away, gravel spewing from under the straining tires. The vehicle vanished into the trees.

The pickup driver ran to Alex and June. He wore a grimy black ball cap and ragged plaid shirt over oil spotted jeans.

"Hey, is everyone okay? I saw you spin out there." He spied the rifle and stopped so suddenly his arms flailed to keep his balance. Hands raised, he backed away. "Oh, hey, I don't want any trouble, man."

June held out her wrists, still bound by the nylon rope. "Please, help us. We were being kidnapped." She gestured at Alex. "See, he's tied up, too. You've got to help us."

"I'll give you the gun," Alex said. "You take it. The kidnappers are in the Jeep. Make sure they don't get out."

The Good Samaritan hesitated. "You put that gun down, I'll think about it."

Alex lowered the rifle to the ground and stepped away, drawing June with him. "Come and get it. But you've got to make sure those two don't get out of the Jeep."

The man picked up the gun using the tips of his fingers.

His caution made Alex wonder if he'd done the right thing, surrendering the weapon. "Have you ever used a rifle before?"

"Of course I have." The man looked affronted. He grasped the weapon firmly and straightened his back.

"Don't you worry none, I'll take care of them." He peered inside the Jeep where Tabitha and Fleetham still lay. "They were kidnapping you?" he asked incredulously.

"It's a long story." Alex sighed. "I work for the Ministry of Environment. I have identification if you want. But first, do you have a knife or something, so we can get this rope off?"

"In the cab. Glove box." Alex started toward the truck, its chrome gleaming. "Don't get any blood on the seat."

****

Events moved quickly once Alex was able to use his cell phone to call Detective George. The pickup driver kept a wary eye on Tabitha and Fleetham, and was incredibly relieved when RCMP members showed up in full force. He cheerfully gave his name to a constable, patted Alex and June heartily on the back, and headed off in his monstrous truck with a snappy wave.

Numerous officials swarmed over the accident scene, led by the grey-haired, grey-eyed detective, whose name Alex never had learned, accompanied by Detective George and Constable Wendy Hoffarth. June sat in the front seat of a cruiser. Alex leaned over the open door, arms folded on the top frame of the window. He kept an eye on June, who was unnervingly still.

Constable Hoffarth strode up. "It seems one of them got away."

Alex nodded. "The big German guy."

"Schwarz-Silber. Walter Schwarz-Silber." June added quietly.

"It shouldn't take us long to find him," Hoffarth assured her. "These two are nattering away a mile a minute." She hooked a thumb over her shoulder, and Alex looked past her to see Fleetham being helped into a cruiser, while Tabitha was strapped onto a gurney in the back of an ambulance. "We'll take him in now, and as soon as they've fixed her up we'll get a chance at her, as well. We've put out a bulletin for their buddy."

"Can we go home?" June asked. Alex's eyes narrowed. She might look like she was holding it together, but her hand trembled as she brushed hair off her forehead. A paramedic had treated her abraded wrists, wrapping them in white bandages. Alex fingers curled into fists.

"I've been asked to drive you both into the detachment. We need to get your statements."

June closed her eyes. The sign of weakness infuriated Alex even further. "Can't it wait until morning?"

"I'm afraid not."

****

Fatigue deepened the dislocation from reality June had experienced since the accident. Everything seemed unnaturally bright and clear, and the smallest sound echoed in her head. At the detachment, the smell of stale coffee and trapped air was so overwhelming it made her queasy. She answered all questions as if an opaque screen separated her from her interviewers. Not even the news Schwarz-Silber had been arrested pierced the veil covering her.

A pink dawn was beginning to glow over the eastern horizon when she and Alex were allowed to leave.

Alex's Jeep had been towed out of the ditch and impounded for forensic investigation, so Hoffarth called them a cab. Eager for fresh air they stepped out onto the sidewalk and waited in the crisp, early light. A police cruiser pulled up to the station. Schwarz-Silber looked daggers in the back.

He'd been found as he was hurriedly leaving a local hotel. According to Hoffarth, who had brought the news to June, the battle he put up when the police apprehended him had done him no favours.

Alex hugged her to his side. She wrapped her arms around his waist.

Schwarz-Silber was led up the steps, struggling in the grip of two large officers. His face purpled with rage when he saw them. "*Du Hurensohn,*" he spat. "*Bloede Kuh! Gottverdammt!*"

June watched silently until they disappeared into the building, then lifted her head to look at Alex. A bruise stained his skin where the rifle butt had gashed his temple. He studied her with an air of concern. This was the man who loved her, who fought for her, who stood next to her.

With a click the world realigned itself. A taxi pulled up at the curb. She lay her cheek against Alex's, rough with stubble, flush with life.

"Let's go home," she said.

****

They staggered wearily into the house and crashed into June's bed. Alex spooned around her, soaking in her warmth. She dropped into sleep immediately, but he was unable to do the same, despite muscles quivering with fatigue. His brain wouldn't shut down, whirling and spinning with the events of the last few days.

Her head fit perfectly under his chin, the silk of her hair sweeping his chest. He inhaled her scent and snugged her tighter against him.

She was truly amazing. Her resourcefulness, her courage, her strength. It had been nothing but the truth when he told her he had never known anyone like her. Throughout his turbulent youth, bounced from one parent to the other, one stepmother or "uncle" to the next, he had been unable to believe in love, in happily ever after. She had changed all that, with her steadiness, her certainty, her love.

Oddly enough, these new feelings helped him understand his father better. It was an adrenalin rush like no other, this falling in love.

She murmured in her sleep and he smoothed a hand up and down her torso. Restless, she flipped onto her back, making small mewling noises. Her hands plucked at the sheets. She gulped in mouthfuls of air, and her eyes opened, but they were wide and frightened and blank as she stared at some nightmare image.

"Hush, now, hush." He cupped her face in both hands. "Look at me. I need you to look at me. Everything is okay."

Her eyes darted right then left, up then down. She never came fully to consciousness, but he continued to talk to her, calmly, softly, and gradually her breathing eased. Once she'd slipped back into sleep, he nestled down with his arms about her and, at last, followed her into slumber.

****

June floated to the surface the next morning. Golden light drifted through the window, glinting in the hairs on Alex's forearm as it draped over her. His breath fanned the back of her neck. She lay still, reveling in their closeness.

"I love you."

She twitched, startled, then turned her head to smile at him. "And I love you. What a wonderful way to wake up."

He rolled onto his back and shifted her so she stretched out above him. "I can think of a better way." With a hand on her nape, he guided her down so he could nibble her lower lip. She moaned, deepened the kiss and relaxed into him.

Their lovemaking was languorous, touches and tastes, sips and sighs. She skimmed through clouds of desire, her mind hazy, passion simmering. Alex's hands glided over her, into her, everywhere, and when she crested the first time it was a long, slow swell that left her gasping.

He slipped into her. Their lips clung, tongues sliding against each other. With long strokes he brought them both closer and closer, in heart, in mind, in body.

And when they shuddered together in that final, wrenching moment, he whispered her name as she called out to him.

She lay sprawled on top of him, her face buried in his neck. He smelled wonderful, male and woodsy and...hers.

"Will you marry me?"

She could have sworn her heart stopped beating. She might have even gone blind for a second. Lifting her head from his shoulder she gazed down at him, flabbergasted. "Marry you? As in a white wedding and 'til death do us part?"

"Oh, is that what it means?" he teased, and earned himself a sharp poke in the ribs. His laughter rippled out.

She sat up, knees on either side of his hips, hands fisted. “Don’t say it if you don’t mean it,” she warned. “Because I won’t let you change your mind. If you’re not in it forever, don’t believe in forever, I’ll hunt you down and kill you.”

He answered with a reckless light in his eye. “I’m good with that. I don’t want to go another day without knowing you are mine, really and truly, forever.”

Pressure built at the back of June’s throat. She allowed herself to hope.

“You are the most incredible woman I have ever met. You’re strong, capable, independent.” He reached up and stroked a finger down the side of her neck, over the upper swell of her breast, across her nipple. She shivered and splayed her hands on his chest. “And when I touch you, you take me places I’ve never been before. I want to love you, and work with you, and fight with you...and make babies with you. I want to marry you.”

This time the tears did spill over. She rubbed them furiously off her cheeks. “I hate this. I hate that I’m crying, when I’m so happy. I love you.” She threw herself onto him and he grunted, then wrapped his arms around her and crushed his mouth to hers. It was a declaration, it was a promise, it was a future.

A word about the author...

Writing and reading have long been ways for Brenda to keep sane. She is thrilled to have actually finished writing a book, let alone have it published. She lives in British Columbia with her husband and three children (all of whom are taller than her) and various finny and furry pets.

Find her on Twitter, Facebook and at www.brendamargriet.com.

CPSIA information can be obtained at www.ICGtesting.com
Printed in the USA
LVOW012132060213

318787LV00005B/13/P

9 781612 177588